An Unexpected Romance

S.B.Roth

ISBN-979852545952
Cover design by: Jessica Randall
Editor: Rachel Garber
Library of Congress Control Number: 2018675309
Printed in the United States of America

To MY small town . . . Population 3998
There's no place like home

Contents

One

Summer was coming to a close, and Rylee wasn't sure if she was ready to have Tyler start school. He was so small for his age. All the other five years olds were at least six inches taller. He only weighed three pounds and two ounces at his birth, but he had grown and finally ended up ALMOST hitting the chart at the pediatrician's office at one percent. His pediatrician always told her, "He'll grow, Rylee. Don't worry; he won't be tiny forever."

Rylee knew she was right, but it was so hard. They had enjoyed everything this summer. Tyler especially loved playing T-ball. It was his first year, and he did pretty well. He was excited about the choir at the church. He'd been in the preschool choir and loved it. Now, as he said, "Mommy, it's with big kids!"

Rylee laughed, "Yes, really big kids!"

Rylee would start her new job when school began. She was a nurse and would be a school nurse at Waterstown Middle School in Waterstown, Texas. With Tyler at the primary and Rylee at the middle school, she would be able to drop him off on her way to work, and their days off would be the same. She was more excited than Tyler.

It had taken her a long time to become a nurse, move to a new town, and start a new job. Tyler was her gift from God. She had given him back to God when he was born. She hadn't been healthy during her pregnancy. The father treated her with callus caring, blaming her for all his problems. Beating her whenever the mood struck and staying either drugged or drunk. Her family did little to intervene. They didn't even want to see Tyler when he was born. She had "disgraced" them, they said.

The father and Rylee had never married. She was only sixteen when she found out she was pregnant. It was a long story that she didn't share much, but she moved in with the older boy, and the abuse began. Walking out before Tyler was born was necessary to her living and thriving.

She had nothing. At least not until she encountered Jesus at a revival in a tent meeting three weeks before Tyler was born. She had gone in with nothing but the baby in her belly. When Rylee walked out, she had Jesus in her heart. When she left the tent, she told Jesus that she would give her son to him, just like Hannah, because of His saving grace. She didn't look back.

Rylee had found a shelter for women. They had cared for her and the newborn. She studied and got her GED which allowed her to enter college. They took care of Tyler when she started nursing school. The women had shown her how to apply for loans and scholarships. Two years later, Rylee graduated as valedictorian and was admired by many for her perseverance.

She became a registered nurse and worked in the small community hospital right outside of Waterstown. The church had found her a small home, and it was a perfect place to honor God and raise her son.

Tyler grew up healthy. Rylee had made enough to feed them, pay for babysitting, and clothe them. Now she wanted to be close to him even when she was at work. The pay wasn't as good, but God had assured her He was still in charge. She reminded everyone always that all she had accomplished was all the Lord's doing. She was doing what He had opened.

Tyler woke early on that first day, ready to go. "Mommy, get up. We need to get ready for school. Mommy, get up!"

Rylee rolled over and grabbed her little one and pulled him up into her bed. "Surely we have time for a minute of snuggles." She laughed as she tickled and tickled him, dropping kisses on his forehead and goosing his neck.

"Oh, Mommy! No! Stop! We got to get dressed!" Tyler was adamant!

"Tyler, school does not start for two more hours. We will have plenty of time. Chill out, boy." Rylee got up, grabbed her robe, and headed to the kitchen. Breakfast was on the agenda and then packing a lunch for both of them.

"I want pancakes. Okay, Mommy?" Tyler loved pancakes, but only with butter. He wasn't much of a sweet eater.

"I think I can manage a few pancakes for my favorite little man," she as she poured the pancakes in different shapes.

When she was finished she told him, "I'm going to take a shower. Be sure you finish your breakfast, and I'll be done in a minute." This was the usual morning routine. Better to keep it simple, she thought. It would be difficult enough when she dropped him off. The school had a strict no-parent policy on the first day to keep the crying to a minimum.

The shower was so good with a blast of hot water. The soap scent of peaches and cream with a hint of mint relaxed Rylee. Jumping out of the shower, she towel-dried her long auburn brown hair and put it up in a bun. That would keep it out of the way. Slacks and a button-up shirt was the outfit for the day along with a pair of new tennis shoes. She was ready for business. She put her lanyard around her neck and was ready to go.

Tyler had started dressing, but Rylee stopped him and made him wash his face and brush his teeth, then put on his shirt. Finally, he got to put on the shark T-shirt that he had picked out all by himself. Like most five-year olds, he was fascinated by sharks. Brushing his unruly, curly blond hair, she was reminded of his non-existent father. Tyler had never asked any questions, and she dreaded the day.

Stopping in front of the school, the teacher came and opened the car door, giving Tyler a high five as he got out.

"Don't worry, Mommy. They'll take good care of me," he promised, then he closed the door and walked off.

Rylee lost it. He's too, little, but he feels all grown up, she thought. Soon he won't need me anymore.

The car behind her honked, urging her to move on. She waved and continued her drive to the middle school about two blocks away. Parking and grabbing her purse, she headed into the building. Her badge unlocked the door, and she was in her office and ready for the day.

"God use this day for Your glory," she said as she opened the nurse's office.

By noon Rylee had greeted over one hundred parents wanting a variety of information from athletic forms to shot information. Rylee wasn't sure she had ever spoken that much! A single dad had come in with his daughter, unsure what to do.

"Hi, this is my daughter, Marcie Hunt. She's new, and I need to make sure she has it all together 'cause I don't!" He laughed. "She's in the seventh grade. She'd like to do band or athletics maybe; I just don't know."

"I only work on medical forms. Why don't you fill out these forms, and then you can talk to the counselor about scheduling."

"Thank you, that would be great." Marcie looked embarrassed at her dad's lack of school knowledge.

"Marcie, would you like to speak with Ms. Bates, our scheduling counselor? Since you didn't preregister she can help you choose from the options available."

"Thank you, I would like that. Dad, well, he doesn't know what's going on!" Marcie smiled like the little mother she appeared to be.

Rylee took Marcie across the hall to the counseling office.

"Mr. Hunt, have you completed the forms?" she asked as she reentered her office. He was just sitting there, pen in hand but not writing.

"Oh, no. I was thinking how much Marcie had grown since . . . oh, never mind. Give me a minute."

"Just bring them to my desk when you're ready." Rylee wondered what had him so occupied.

The rest of the day went fine. Kids were in and out, teachers were scheduling days Rylee could come to classes to teach a health lesson. The regular everyday routine for a small school. Around two-thirty, Rylee left to pick up Tyler from kindergarten. Arriving right on time, she found Tyler talking with a little red-headed girl while they sat on the steps waiting. The teacher was standing nearby.

"Tyler, are you ready?" Calling out from the car window.

Tyler looked up, "No, Mommy, not until Susie's daddy comes to pick her up. She's scared, and I told her I'd take care of her."

Rylee smiled at her son and the teacher nearby. Her son the caretaker! "Is it all right if I sit down with you?" she asked, parking and getting out of the car.

"Of course. Susie, this is my Mommy."

"Hello, Susie. I'm sure your daddy will be here soon. I'll wait with you." Susie kept watching the road not talking to anyone.

"Daddy! Daddy!" Susie began yelling and jumping up and down. "I'm here, Daddy!"

Rylee looked up and saw a tall man with blond hair walking her way. He was with the little girl from the middle school, Marcie.

"I'm right here, sugar. Let's go." Susie jumped up and ran to her daddy.

"Mr. Hunt. I had no idea you had a little one in kindergarten. This is my son Tyler."

Tyler hid behind his mommy's legs and gave a small "Hi." Sometimes he was a little shy with new people.

Mr. Hunt stretched out his hand, and Tyler shook it. "It's nice to see you again, Ms. Abrams. Nice to meet you Tyler." Bending down, he picked up Susie and said goodbye.

"Can we go now, Mommy?" Tyler was jumping up and down, ready to leave.

As they walked to the car, Tyler told his mommy all about his day. He learned the letter O and the sounds it could make. Tyler was so proud. Then he began telling her about Susie. She had cried all day because she missed her daddy, and he was the only one in class that could get her to stop.

"Why was she crying so much. Did she not feel well?" Rylee was a little lost on why the teacher didn't help the poor child.

"Susie said she didn't have a mommy. I told her that was all right. She could have you. Then she said, since I didn't have a daddy, I could have her daddy, and then it was all okay. Well, it was all right, until after school when her daddy wasn't around and she started crying again." Tyler just frowned for a second before smiling really big. "I'll remind her tomorrow."

"That was mighty generous of you, Tyler." Rylee said as she hugged her son. Tyler was a good kid; no need to upset the apple cart! After dinner, they sat down and went over all the papers he had brought home. Coloring page options on the computer were offered as well. Rylee didn't feel any pressure at Tyler's age to worry about "homework"; she figured they'd see how things went the next few weeks.

"Mommy, I'm so tired. Do you care if I go to bed early?" Tyler was yawning so big she could see his tonsils. Not used to the routine of school could wear anyone out.

"Mommy's tired too. I'll get you in bed, and I'll follow real soon." She began reading him one of his favorite children's books, but he fell asleep before they finished.

It had been a long day for everyone. The house that Rylee and Tyler lived in was an old two bedroom. Rylee had spent time cleaning and painting and when they moved in she felt happier than she had in a while. Entering the front door, the living area was small and had two doors coming off of it, one led to the bedrooms and one to the kitchen. The hall which connected the bedrooms to the kitchen had a nice big bathroom. The backyard wasn't big but it had a nice picket fence around it and in front yard was an old oak tree, at least a hundred years old. As Rylee sat in the living area, she thought of the cute little redhead without a momma. Wonder where she is? Maybe they are divorced. Rylee sat up thinking, Oh, I hope she didn't die. That would be so difficult for a little girl. It had been six years since she had seen her mom. Six years since she had been kicked out.

Two

The alarm went off with what seemed like a loud foghorn. Rylee sat up in bed, looked at the clock, and got up reluctantly. It was only Wednesday, she thought. Summer had been a lazy time, and it was hard getting used to the routine. Slipping on her house shoes, she went into Tyler's room only to find his bed empty. After her heart skipped about three beats, she realized the noise she was hearing was the TV in the other room.

"You know you aren't allowed TV until the afternoon, Tyler Weston Abrams," she said, walking over and shutting it off.

He knew he was in trouble when she used his middle name! "I know, but you were still asleep, so I didn't think you'd care."

"Well, I do. Go wash up and get dressed. Come in the kitchen when you're finished and have breakfast. We need to get on our way!" she instructed.

They had been in school only two days, and things were anything but routine in the Abrams household this morning. Tyler couldn't get enough of his cute little redhead friend. He had talked about her all evening.

Rylee received a thank you note the next day from Mr. Hunt. He was appreciative of Tyler taking care of Susie. She had thought that was very nice of him.

The past two days were full for Rylee. It was amazing to hear how many students had headaches and stomachaches. Parents called to see if their children were all right because they had the sniffles that morning. Then there were the children who weren't okay, the ones who no one called about, the ones that could have been her at that age. Those were the ones she worried about. Skipping school, some were caught vaping in the bathroom, and the way they dressed it was apparent the parents weren't keeping their eyes on the kids. And that was the first week of school.

The second week of school, she started a program for each grade level. The first week they discussed why we brush our teeth, take baths, keep our clothes washed. It seemed a little elementary, but the kids really were unaware of body odor and bad breath. It was fun. The kids would ask some of the silliest and then some of the most adult questions. She really enjoyed her time with them. She also knew the teachers enjoyed her giving them a little break.

One morning, several weeks after school had begun, she received a call from a parent complaining that their daughter was sitting next to someone who coughed and was afraid of getting sick. Rylee almost laughed into the phone at the lady on the other end. She would get two or three calls like this as the weeks moved on. She knew parents were protective, but this seemed like an irrational extent.

The friendship between Tyler and Susie had blossomed into a playdate at school and one when Susie and Marcie went home with Rylee, but most were at the school when Susie's daddy was late picking her up. When Tyler started choir a few weeks later, Rylee called Mr. Hunt to see if Susie could join.

"Hi, David. This is Rylee Abrams again. Tyler goes to the church on Tuesdays for Children's choir, and he would love it if Susie could join him. Marcie could also go to the middle school choir group if you think she would like it."

"They might, Rylee. I'll talk to both girls and see how they feel. Can I call you back tonight after they get home from school?"

"Sure, I'll be looking forward to hearing from you." Rylee thought about how nice David was, but he was quiet. She had noticed from the papers he had completed that he worked at one of the horse ranches in the area. He was much too large to be a jockey, so she looked into the ranch's website and found that he was a veterinarian specializing in quarter horses. Rylee thought it was interesting to learn that some ranches hire their own vets.

Later that night, David called and said both girls were excited to join. Rylee suggested that she would just take Marcie and they'd go pick up Tyler and Susie from school. She would drop them off at the church and make sure they knew where to go.

"Choir usually runs from three-thirty until five. After choir, they have a snack and a quick devotional, and I'll bring them home afterward."

"I can pick them up, along with Tyler, and bring him by your place. Where exactly do I pick them up?" David offered.

They shared information, and it was settled. Rylee would take them, and David would return them. She knew the kids would have fun.

The next day she picked up Tyler and the girls and took them to choir. David arrived to drop them off around five-thirty.

"I hope the girls had a good time." Rylee smiled at David.

"Oh, they most certainly did. I couldn't seem to get them to be quiet on the way home," David laughed at the fun they must have had. They talked nonstop since getting in the car. "I want to thank you for inviting them."

"No problem. If you'd like to come to church on Sunday, the service starts at nine and Sunday School begins at ten-fifteen. We'd love to have you join us."

"Thank you, I'll think about it." David turned and left.

Such a nice man. Rylee wondered what happened to his wife.

David walked down the steps of Rylee's porch. Rylee was the only friend David had made since moving to Waterstown. She was a beautiful young woman, emphasis on the young. But he wasn't looking for a relationship right now, he only wanted friendship. The girls needed that interaction with another woman to help with the loss of their mom. Rylee might be the one to help.

He would be out of town for a week soon and would either have to pull the kids out to travel with him or find someone to watch them. He was going to five different ranches to look at mares that were for sale. The owners wanted his opinion of each. Did he know Rylee well enough to ask her? He'd think about it, but as it happened, he didn't have to think about it for long.

The following day as David was getting the girls ready for school Marcie had a big question.

"Daddy, while you're gone next week, can we stay at Ms. Abrams's house. She is so nice. She reminds me of mommy. Please, Daddy."

"Listen, sugar, I can ask, but she may have other plans. I'll call her today and see what she says, all right?" David wasn't looking forward to the call. In fact, he was a little embarrassed that he had to make it.

About that time, Susie came running into the kitchen. She had lost her two front teeth during the summer and her permanent teeth hadn't started growing in yet. She was whistling through them loudly whenever she could, "Phwwwwwhht, Daddy, Marcie says we can stay with Tyler's mommy while you're gone. Thank you, Daddy, thank you," she said, hugging him ever so tightly around the legs. Then began whistling again, "Phwwwwwhht."

"I don't know yet, Susie. I need to speak with her today. Then I'll let you know," he responded hugging his little daughter as she jumped into his arms.

"Oh, Daddy, I know she'll want us to stay!" Susie kissed her daddy and hopped down.

Later that night, as David looked at his wife's picture, he felt that she was saying it was time to move on. It had been over two years, but his heart felt like it was just yesterday. The girl's hearts were mending much quicker. They still cried sometimes at bedtime when they said their prayers. But they were losing the memory of her; at least Susie, who was only three when she passed, was forgetting her. David was heartbroken when Susie would ask if her mommy had loved her, sometimes she wanted to talk about what they did together since she no longer had any recollection.

The next morning, David called the school and asked to speak with the nurse. "Is Ms. Abrams in her office?" He asked.

"No, she's in a classroom right now. May I help you?" The general secretary answered.

"Is there any way I could leave her a voice mail?"

"Yes, call back and then hit one-one; that's her extension. You'll get a voice mailbox."

"Thank you for your help."

David called back and hit one-one and was sent to Rylee's voice mailbox. "Hi, Rylee, this is David. I . . . need to ask a favor if you could call me back at my regular number, please." He felt sure she would return his call later.

∞∞∞

Listening to her messages, Rylee wondered what kind of favor David needed. They were just now on a first-name basis, and they'd known each other all of four weeks. She'd call him after lunch since she was on lunch duty this week.

Walking into the cafeteria was eye-opening. One hundred students trying to eat lunch simultaneously in a short period could get hectic and loud. Still, the principal handled it with calmness and strength. Approaching Rylee, he asked, "Is this your first week on lunch duty, Ms. Abrams?"

"Why yes, it is, Mr. Keene. How can you tell?"

"Just that deer in the headlights look!" he laughed. "It's all right. Most days are like this one. Some get worse, and others are better. Just take your week in stride. If you'll just walk among the tables, keep the children somewhat quiet and see if anyone needs anything. One from a table may leave to go to the bathroom, but only one at a time."

"Thank you." Rylee began walking around the tables that littered the small cafeteria. As she walked by Marcie, the little girl caught her attention.

"Ms. Abrams, has my dad spoken to you yet about Susie and me staying with you next week?"

Rylee raised her eyebrows, "I have a message to call him. What are you talking about?"

"Oh, my dad has to go out of town next week, and we wanted to stay with you, so we asked him to ask you. He wasn't too excited, but we told him you wouldn't care. You love us already."

Although it was true that she loved them, she wasn't sure she had enough room for them to stay. She'd pray about it before returning David's call. When she got back to the office, she found a sixth-grader throwing up in her trash. Calling the young man's parents, they said they would be there as quick as one of them could get off work. She made Henry comfortable on the bed and gave him a cool rag and a bucket to use. Partially closing the door, she made the return call. No answer. She left a short message saying she'd call him back in an hour.

∞ ∞ ∞

David had been so busy all day that he wasn't able to get back with Rylee. He had seen when she had called, but he hadn't had time to return the call. It was Wednesday afternoon, and David needed to confirm what the girls were going to do. As he pulled into the parking lot at the middle school, he saw Rylee walking to her car with Tyler and his girls.

"Rylee," he called to her, "Rylee Abrams!"

Rylee couldn't see who was calling her. She stopped and looked around, finally seeing David at the other side of the parking lot. Waving to him, she began to walk in his direction. The girls began running to him.

"Hey, David, I tried to call you but no answer." She had forgotten to call again.

"That's fine. Do you have room for two extra people in your house?" Let's get this out of the way, he thought.

"Marcie told me you were going out of town, and they wondered if they could stay with Tyler and me. My place is small. They'd have to share a bunk bed in Tyler's room. Would that be okay with them?"

"Why don't I bring them over tonight and let them see for themselves. I can always take the girls with me. They're the ones that brought this up!" He laughed as Rylee opened her mouth to respond.

"We go to church on Wednesday nights. I have a Bible study, and then Tyler has youth group. We won't be home until eight."

"That's all right. We can come over tomorrow night if you are free."

"That's fine, or you could stop by the house and go to Bible study, and the girls could go to youth group. Then they'd see what the house looked like."

David wasn't sure about all the church activities, but if that's what it took, then okay. "Sounds good. I'll be there with the girls about five-thirty."

"Make it five. We eat at church also."

"I suppose we can be there at five. See you then."

Both got into their cars and headed in different directions. This was the closest David had come to dating since his wife died.

∞∞∞

That night after Tyler had gone to bed, Rylee curled up on the couch and thought about the precious hours when Tyler was born. No reason to go back, except she had been a little nostalgic since she had met the Hunt girls. Rylee had always wanted Tyler to have a sister or brother. She had been an only child. An only unwanted child. No wonder she went looking for love in all the wrong places. She laughed softly at the song pun. She did that a lot — found a song to fit her situation.

Clint Owens had been the stud football player and she, just like all the other girls, was in love with him. Clint was best at flirting, and he found a moment to talk to her whenever he could. Her parents didn't allow her to date, but that didn't keep her from seeing him. What she didn't know was that he was seeing all the other girls behind the bleachers, in the same place he would always meet her. This led to some pretty heavy kissing.

"I love you, Rylee," he would say this to her all the time. "You're the only one for me. I want to marry you when we get out of school."

She believed him. Rylee was so desperate for someone to love her that she believed whatever he said. She didn't realize he saw her as an easy mark. The way she came at his beck and call told him all he needed to know. But that didn't last long, and when she realized she was pregnant, her parents kicked her out. Clint graduated from high school, and they ended up living in an old rundown garage apartment. He rarely worked, drank way too much, and his drug habit got out of hand. One night after a long day of being hungover, Clint had come in yelling, pushing her around, and calling her foul names. When she tried to fight back, he began hitting her with his fists, bruising all over her arms and cuts on her face. She couldn't take it anymore, so she walked out. She had more self-respect than this. She didn't need him. She tried to find a job, but she had no car, no clothes, and no way to make it to work . . . and she was pregnant. She did her best to finish school, but she had a year left when she quit.

She went into labor three weeks later. She had Tyler — one look at those perfectly kissable cheeks, the soft cry he made as he was placed on her chest — it was the best day of her life.

Three

"All right, girls, do you think you can sleep on that bed for a week together with Tyler sleeping on the top?" Rylee was giving David a full tour of the tiny house after church.

"I think they'd be okay. The girls aren't huge, so this bed should work." David said. "Girl's, what do you think?"

"Yes, Daddy, we can do it, so can we stay with Ms. Abrams? PLEASE!"

Tyler got off his bunk. "Mr. Hunt, I'd like to have Susie and Marcie stay. Would it be okay?" He gave David his best smile.

David smiled. Tyler was the sweetest little boy. Rylee was raising a fine young man. He wondered where the dad was, "Won't you get tired of having girls around, Tyler?"

"I always have my mom around, and she's a girl. I've gotten used to it."

Rylee laughed and ruffled his hair.

David thought Rylee was beautiful. He loved her laugh and the smattering of freckles across her cheeks. Gentle was a word David would use for Rylee. Of course, her auburn, wavy hair helped and her beautiful eyes. He smiled at the thought.

"Well, I suppose they can come over Sunday night, and I'll be home by Thursday night or Friday morning. Thank you, Tyler and Rylee, for opening your home."

Jumping up and down, the three kids did somersaults and high kicks all around the room. "Yeah!!"

Rylee and David laughed, reminding them to be careful and slow down. Soon David gathered his girls and headed for the door.

"Tomorrow is a school day, girls. We need to be going. Thank you, Rylee and Tyler, for inviting us to church tonight. It's been a long time, and it reminded me why I need to get back in the groove. See you, and I'll be over around five Sunday evening to drop off the girls."

"We're looking forward to it. I'll see you then if not before. Marcie, I'll see you at school tomorrow." She hugged the girls goodbye and watched them leave with a smile on her face.

The days were busy. Rylee was working through the files of every student at the middle school, checking shot records. She'd much rather be in the classroom with the children, but it wasn't scheduled for another three weeks. Every day brought at least one or two kids to her office with headache, cough, sore throat, or just generally not feeling well. Calling parents and meeting parents, she was beginning to feel at home in the district. Rylee was so glad they had moved to this tiny rural town in Texas several years ago. It was close enough to a big city if she needed it but small enough to feel cozy whenever she went out.

Five o'clock Sunday was fast approaching, and she needed to buy enough groceries to sustain the new members of her household. She had asked Marcie what they like to eat, but she gave only a few ideas. Mostly eggs and pancakes. Surely they hadn't been living on that only for the last several years. After school on Friday, she and Tyler ran to a neighboring community to buy groceries. Her list was longer than expected, so it took a little extra time. Marcie had also shared their love of hot dogs and hamburgers, but their favorite food was chicken fried steak and gravy with mashed potatoes. Rylee had never made chicken fried steak, but she would try and wing it if possible.

Walking up and down the aisles, Tyler would put in, and Rylee would take out, "Tyler, we are not buying a bunch of junk. Understood?"

"Yes, ma'am." He did his famous frowny face, but it didn't help. He still had to put it back.

Turning to the next aisle, Rylee was busy talking to Tyler and when she bumped the basket of a fellow shopper. Looking up, she saw David and smiled.

"Fancy meeting you here." Rylee couldn't get over how good he smelled. She hadn't put her finger on what it was, but it was a fragrance that she would always recognize!

"Well, hi, Rylee. Are you stocking up for the weekend?" It was a pleasant surprise to see Rylee.

"Why yes, I am. At least I'm trying too. I'm having to keep Tyler from dumping junk into the cart."

"Well, Tyler, if you ask me, a little junk is all right too."

"David, don't encourage him, please." She laughed, giving David a motherly frown.

"Carry on, team Abrams. I will see you on Sunday evening." As he began to leave, Rylee spoke up.

"Where are the girls?"

"OH NO," he said, smacking his head. "I forgot to get them from school!" David looked at Rylee's face as it fell in horror. He gave her a goofy grin; the priceless look was exactly the reason he had said what he had.

"They're next door eating ice cream waiting on me. They hate grocery shopping. One of the girls I know from the stables is watching them."

Rylee laughed. This guy was opening up, and he was one of the good guys. She could learn to trust him.

Checking out, she saw David going into the store next door to get the girls. When they walked out, they were accompanied by a tall blonde.

∞∞∞

Saturday hurried by in a blur. David had checked on each horse in the stables, drove to another part of the ranch and checked those horses. All seemed to be in a good place for him to leave on Sunday. The girls were excited. They hadn't been overnight for so long. Their mom had always been there, but it went so fast after cancer diagnosis, and she was gone.

He planned to attend church services in the morning and take the girls on a quick picnic before he had to be at Rylee's to drop them off. They would ride up into the woods near the lake and spend an hour looking for rocks, pinecones, and bird feathers. Those were the three things the girls always came home with, and then they painted rocks and pinecones, gluing the feathers to them. Occasionally they would take time to make Ojo de Dios, God's Eye. His office was full of these productive artworks of nature.

"Daddy, can we ask Tyler to go on our picnic today?" Susie was crushing hard on Tyler. If they were any older, David would worry.

"We don't know if Tyler can ride a horse or not. Maybe we can wait and ask them, and he can come next time. Is that okay?"

"Sure. That's okay." Her sweet little freckled face was down-turned, but he hugged her, and she came out of the pout.

Getting the girls ready for church was a new experience. He and Clara had attended church, but they only had Marcie, and Clara had gotten her ready. By the time Susie was old enough to attend, Clara was ill, and they just didn't go. When she died, David was so angry at God that he refused to go to the one place where he had always found peace — in the arms of Jesus.

He was ready. The girls were in choir. He had started the Bible study on Wednesday, now the next step was Sunday services. Just listening to the Word would help to heal his soul.

Walking into the church gave him a sense of belonging. He hadn't felt this way for a while, and he knew it was a good thing. The praise band was rehearsing before the service, and he saw the preacher playing his guitar on stage with everyone else. He had met Pastor Park at Bible Study. Based on how the study had gone, he knew the sermon would be good.

The sermon was over Galatians 1:11. Where did Paul's Bible-based knowledge come from? The pastor reminded us in his sermon that Paul's life was not perfect. He was a Jewish man who persecuted Jews. He was zealous in his job until he met Christ. David thought back to his years before Christ. Paul was right. We all must meet Jesus. We must remember how our lives were before we accepted Him and how they had changed.

Leaving the service that morning, David knew he needed to change some things in his life. Reaching out to those around him would be a good start. Seeing Rylee and Tyler as they left, he waved and told them they would be over at five.

"Why can't we go talk to them?" Marcie was now doing all the questioning. "If we're not going to Sunday School, then I want to talk to them, please."

"Marcie, we need to get home and get changed for our picnic. You're usually so ready to go horseback riding. What's different?"

"I just need to speak with Ms. Abrams for a minute." Looking around, she no longer saw them. "Oh, never mind, they're gone now." She stomped off, headed to the truck.

When David and Susie got into the truck, he stopped and looked at Marcie. "Marcie, never are you to stomp your foot at me or speak to me in that tone of voice. Understood?"

"Yes, sir. Daddy it was girl stuff. I'm sorry." Marcie was still upset, but she knew she had overstepped.

The home they lived in was a sweet two-story log cabin, about ten miles out of town. It was provided by the ranch owners for the vet and his family to live. Four bedrooms, four bathrooms, family room, dining and kitchen. The kitchen was the top of the line. The kids had the entire field to play, but it was close to the barn and stalls for the horses. Occasionally the smell could be overpowering in the summer heat. Even though the stalls were kept immaculate, there was still that smell.

Once they got home, everyone changed clothes, and they met in the barn to saddle their horses. Even Susie had to help. She couldn't put the saddle on her pony, but she could carry the blanket and cinch the buckle. Susie's pony was just her size, about ten hand height, a chestnut brown, and a little older with no skittish tendencies. She had been riding Brownie for about a year. Marcie rode a blonde Palomino about thirteen hand height. She loved Girl, which was a strange name, but what Marcie wanted to name her. Girl was a calm horse and fit Marcie perfectly. David always checked both of the girls' work to make sure they were safe. His horse was old Black Beard. Black Beard was a larger horse since David was taller, but he was still gentle and didn't outrun or get skittish around other horses. The ranch wasn't too far from the lake area. The places they had gone to were always near the water and quite beautiful in the fall. After a brief run with the horses, they then trotted along to find the place they always went near Rock Creek.

Tying the horses to a couple of trees, they sat down on the blanket they had spread out and ate the lunch the main house had put together for them. Everything looked so good: roast beef sandwich, peanut butter and jelly sandwiches, along with chips and cookies and water to drink. Susie always remembered to bring carrots, sugar cubes, and water for the horses, so they also had lunch. The day had turned out a little windy, so they didn't stay too long. The girls quickly found their art materials for the day and added a few dried oak leaves. Bundling them up, they untied the horses, and they were off to the house. They would get ready and then head to Rylee's home about four-thirty.

∞ ∞ ∞

Rylee wasn't sure why she was cleaning the house for two kids. However, she knew that a clean home was always more inviting and she wanted to make sure the girls felt at ease while they stayed with her.

She had planned spaghetti for supper with breadsticks and a salad. Tyler thought that was an excellent first-night dinner.

She changed the sheets on the bed and made sure she had breakfast thought out before the next morning; four lunches to fix in the morning might be her undoing if she didn't plan correctly.

Breathe, girl, breathe. Suddenly her phone rang and shocked her out of her trance. She didn't recognize the number and let it go right to voicemail. As she laid the phone down, the doorbell rang. Ah, she thought, when it rained it poured.

"Hey, guys. Come on in. Are you ready for the chaos of a weeklong sleepover? Tyler, the girls are here." Hugging everyone as they came through the door, she grabbed a suitcase from David and placed it next to the couch. "Do you need a hug too?" She asked jokingly.

"I could probably use one more than the girls!" He was only teasing, but Rylee walked right up and gave him a big motherly hug. Only it didn't feel so motherly to him. Gosh, she smelled good, . . . like lavender, he thought.

"Here are the phone numbers where I can be reached. If you don't connect with one, then try another. Here is a copy of our insurance, and I took the liberty of signing a parental consent form in case someone got hurt. You could make quick decisions for me. I hope that was all right."

"More than all right. I'll keep you posted about how our week goes, but we should be fine. Are you driving or flying?"

"I'm driving. There are three quarter-horse ranches I'll be going to. The furthest is on the west side of New Mexico. Then I'll head back this way. I know everything will be okay, but they are all I have."

"Dad, no worries. I'll love them like I love my own." Rylee knew he was worried. "We can FaceTime you each evening if you want."

"No, just play it by ear. I'm not sure Susie's aware of how long four days can be."

They all followed David back outside and stood on the lawn to wave goodbye.

From a distance, a lone figure stood and watched and wondered what was going on. Turning and walking off, no one even noticed how interested he had been in what was happening.

Four

Monday morning was hectic beyond belief. Marcie didn't want to get up. Susie was up and in bed with Rylee before the alarm, and Tyler wanted a hug and extra snuggles with all the changes taking place in his house. Finally, breakfast was ready, and the three kiddos were ready to go. Rylee sat them on the couch while she picked up their lunches in the kitchen, handed one to each, and corralled them into the car.

"Whew," she said to a coworker when she walked into the school, "it is definitely a difference with three than it was with just my one. I guess by Friday, it will be old hat!"

Lyndzey, her coworker, laughed. "I have enough trouble getting ready with just my two."

"I didn't realize the difference. Tomorrow we will have a different tactic. I hope!" Laughing, Rylee heard her phone ring and went to answer it. "Rylee Abrams, nurse, may I help you?"

"Ah, no, I must have dialed the wrong number." The person hung up.

That's strange, thought Rylee. They had to call the main office first to get it transferred to her number. The person must have known who would answer. Well, she was new, so that may have thrown them off guard.

The day went smoothly until noon. Once the last group had eaten lunch, she began to have sixth graders coming in with a tummy ache and throwing up, all symptoms of food problems. They ate something that didn't sit right, and each had eaten in the lunchroom. By three-thirty, there were ten kids from different grades in the nurse's office and parents picking them up.

Rylee and the workers in the lunchroom sat down and went through all the food options for them to eat. After much discussion, they had the ice cream bars narrowed down to the culprit. First, they called all the parents to see if their child had the ice cream bar, then they called the company to look at the batch number in case others called. They promised to be out in the morning to pick up what was left over or the school could just chunk it in the trash.

Picking up Susie and Tyler after school was much easier with Marcie. She got out of the car and went up to meet them and bring them to the car. She got them into the back seat, hooked their seatbelts, and away they went.

"You're the little mother today, Marcie." She immediately realized what she had said. "I'm sorry, Marcie. I don't want you to be sad. You're really the big sister today and every day."

"It's all right, Ms. Abrams. My daddy calls me the little mom at our house. It's a compliment."

Rylee felt a little better.

"Mommy, can we go get ice cream today?"

Rylee laughed. "No ice cream, but how about a root beer? Does that sound good?"

All three yelled, "YES!"

Rylee drove by the nearest drive-through, and they came away with three small root beers and a super large order of fries. Rylee was ready to get home. She was tired and still had supper to cook.

Pulling into the drive, she noticed a man about her age walking in front of the house. She'd never seen him in the neighborhood before. Big guy, looked like a football player. Maybe he was home from school for a visit. She couldn't see his face. He looks like . . . One of the girls pulled her out of her thoughts.

"Can we play in the backyard?" Susie was itching to get outside.

"Do you have homework?" Rylee knew they needed to read, but they could play for a little while.

"I got to read, maybe for a minute. Can we play?" Susie was pleading.

"Okay, stay in the back. No over the fence or in the front today."

They agreed, and Marcie and Rylee went into the house.

∞∞∞

Clint walked away so Rylee wouldn't recognize him. He hadn't changed much, just lost some weight and muscle mass. He was still a big guy. He had seen her picture in the local newspaper about being a new employee of the school district. He couldn't believe they ended up in the same town again.

Six years had been a long time. Clint had quit the drugs, went to anger management classes after beating up his ex-wife, and spent a few months in jail. Once he was out, he went back to school and got a certificate for construction work. He earned himself a good job traveling with a company and building large offices. Clint had just finished a five-story building in a neighboring town. He was hoping to become a foreman on the next job.

He'd known he had a kid out there, but he never really cared until now. So he had a boy, and he had blond curly hair just like him. He was somewhat little, but he'd grow up big and maybe he would be just like his old dad. He still didn't know how he'd introduce himself to the kid. Maybe he better talk to the mom first. Something told him Rylee was going to be difficult if he wanted to see him. He could understand. Clint had treated her horribly. He still had some penitence to pay for that too.

Clint needed to hurry back to work. He told his boss he needed to run an errand, and it had already been forty-five minutes. Jumping back into his truck, he took off across town to his work.

∞∞∞

Rylee looked out back while she and Marcie worked on dinner. Marcie had finished all her homework immediately after going inside and moved on to help Rylee in the kitchen. She was turning out to be quite the cook.

"Ms. Abrams."

"Rylee, just call me Rylee."

"I need to ask you a question, and I'm kind of embarrassed."

Rylee stopped what she was doing and sat at the table. "What can I help you with, Marcie?"

"I don't know how to ask my dad, so I thought you might be able to help me. I mean, I hear a lot at school, but I never know whether to believe it or not. You know so many girls tell stories to impress people."

"Well, I'm a girl, and I'm not looking to impress anyone. Fire away." Rylee wondered what this was all about.

"I need a bra. I mean, I'm not very big, but the coach said I had to wear one to school and I don't have one. Can you help me get one? I wanted to tell my dad, but he's always so busy."

Rylee took a deep sigh of relief it was an easy topic. "Why, of course, I can. Why don't I talk to the coach, and she can let you out of class early, and we'll run to the store before we pick up Susie and Tyler."

Marcie hugged Rylee. "Oh, thank you, Ms. . . . I mean Rylee."

About that time, Susie and Tyler came running in and said they were starving. While they washed up, Rylee and Marcie set the table and put the food out to eat. It was a blessed meal as everyone talked and told what they had been doing that day, lots of laughter and lots of joy.

Marcie laughed, "This has been so fun. My mommy used to tell me that joy was where Jesus lived. So, Jesus has been right here with us all day!"

They had forgotten to call their dad Monday night, so they made a quick call to him before school on Tuesday.

"Daddy!" they yelled. "We're having so much fun."

David was happy to hear from them. "I'm so glad. What are you doing today?"

Everyone yelled, "SCHOOL!"

"I forgot! Sorry! Have a good day. Let me speak with Rylee, please."

Handing the phone off to Rylee, she said, "Hello David. I'm sorry we forgot to call last night. All is well, and they're waiting for your return to tell you all about it on Friday."

"I'll try to be there early. You all better get to school. See you then. Bye"

"Bye." Rylee walked off humming, "Bye, Bye, Birdie". . . another one of her go-to songs.

The following two days flew by as the children had school and choir, then on Wednesday, they attended church and youth group. The girls had spent some FaceTime with their dad before church. Rylee thought Susie was getting a little cranky without her daddy around.

One evening, she cuddled up to Rylee and asked, "Is my daddy coming home?"

"Well, of course, he is, sweetheart. He should be home on Friday. What makes you think he isn't coming home?"

"My mommy went away and never came back. Is that what my daddy is doing?"

Rylee hugged her tight. "Not at all. You got to talk with your daddy on the phone earlier, and we can call him right now if you want to. He'll be home before you know it."

"I think I love you, Ms. Abrams. You're just like a mommy. You smell good, and your hugs are perfect." Susie started to cry. "If daddy doesn't come home, can I live with you?"

Rylee's heart broke in pieces. "Oh honey, you can stay with me forever if that's something that you want. I love you too." Picking her up, she held her tight until she fell asleep. She took Susie to her bed and tucked her in. "You can sleep with me tonight if you want."

Susie nodded her head. Rylee laid down next to her and rubbed her back until Susie was lightly snoring, just like she did with Tyler when he was upset.

∞ ∞ ∞

Friday finally arrived, and David picked the girls up from school. They were so excited when they got to the house to pick up their bags.

"Look, Ms. Abrams, my daddy is here." Susie had a smile that made her whole face shine.

Rylee whispered, "I told you he'd be home." Then she gave her a huge hug.

Susie followed suit, "I know!"

They didn't stay long. Eager to get back home, they left shortly after with lots of thank you's and promises to get together again. Finally, it was just Tyler and Rylee. "Did you enjoy having them here, Tyler?"

"It was fun. But I got tired. Company is a lot of work." Tyler sighed and sat down on the couch.

About that time, Rylee's phone rang in the kitchen, and she hurried to answer. "Hello." Once again, there was a hesitation from whoever was calling. "Who is this?"

"Rylee?" the voice on the other end spoke.

"Yes, who is this?" By now, Rylee was hopping mad. "Answer me."

"It's Clint."

Rylee almost fainted, the word 'survivor' came to her mind. Sitting down at the table, she made sure Tyler was in the other room and couldn't hear her. "Why are you calling? How . . . how did you get this number?" She was shaking as she pictured him pushing her around.

"I'm not trying to make any problems, Rylee. I didn't seek you out. I just saw your picture in the paper."

"Yes, well, I started a new job. That doesn't explain why you're calling. It's been years, Clint. I don't want to catch up or anything like that. Leave me alone."

"I want to see the boy."

"The BOY has a name. I knew you had an agenda, Clint." Rylee had been dreading this day; it was only a matter of time before it happened.

"No agenda. Just want to meet Tyler."

"Why now? You didn't care enough five years ago. Why do you care now?" Rylee was over this guy. How could he think that they could pick up where they left off? He abused her and treated her horribly. She wanted to put him back into that little area of her brain that she didn't have to think about.

"He doesn't have to know I'm his dad. I want to meet him. Can we meet at the food court? I'll say I'm an old friend."

"Let me think about it. NO." Then Rylee hung up. Words from one of her favorite praise songs filled her mind: for so long I carried the weight of my past. She was over her past now.

Rylee's hands were shaking. She had gone all these years without thinking about Tyler's father, and now here he was. She didn't know what to do. She would think about it. Let him go where he goes, and maybe he won't call her back. Besides, she was busy this weekend and all next week. She didn't even want Tyler to know this man who had been bent on ruining her life.

"Hey, Mommy," Tyler was calling her from the living room.

Walking back to him, she began smiling, wrapped her arms around him, and gave him a big hug. "Have I told you lately how much I love you, Tyler?" She began singing to him, . . . love lifted me . . .

"Oh, Mommy, you always sing that song to me." Then he flipped on the television to watch cartoons.

Rylee sat down beside him, and while he watched, she tried to find a way out of this mess without Tyler learning who his father was. Without missing a beat, she picked up her phone and called David. He would help her make a decision. He'd know what she should do.

Her call went to voicemail, "Hello, David. It's Rylee. I know you just got home, but I'm making a nice pot roast on Sunday, and I thought you and the girls might like to come for dinner. I have something I need some advice on, so I thought we could talk. Let me know. Bye."

It was late when she crawled into bed. Tyler had fallen asleep in front of the television, and she carried him to bed. She took a long hot shower, and when she got out, she had a message from David confirming dinner on Sunday would be great. Sleep didn't come easy. When it did — it was fitful and nightmarish.

Five

Dinner on Sunday was eventful. The kids would not or could not stop talking about Sunday School. They enjoyed a lunch of roast, potatoes, carrots, and corn on the cob, and then the kids watched television while David helped with the cleanup. It was on the chilly side this day in November, so the kids did not want to go outside.

"You ate very little, Rylee. What's up? What is it you wanted to discuss?" David opened up the issue since it didn't look like Rylee was bringing it up.

"I hate to bother you with this, but you're a man . . ." Rylee began.

David interrupted her, laughing, "Wait, you noticed? Well, I'll be."

Rylee smiled, "Oh hush. I need a father's advice, so you're the only father I have around, so here we go."

"Tell me the problem. Then we can go from there. Ease into it," David said.

"This is hard to ease into. It's about Tyler . . . and his father." Rylee turned her head, so she was looking out the window. "We never married. I was a rebellious type, a teen rebel I guess," she said, laughing at her joke. "I thought he hung the moon when we first started dating in high school. I was so naïve. He was actually with several other girls at the same time. Did I mention I was sixteen?" Rylee stopped to take a deep breath. She hated sharing this with him.

"It's okay, Rylee. Where is he now?"

"I wasn't sure until I got a call from him Friday night. He's right here in town, and he wants to meet Tyler. He's never seen him. He said he doesn't want to tell him who he is, just meet him. David, he's an abuser; he abused me and apparently his ex-wife. He's been in jail. I know people can change. But has he really?"

David realized he needed to be careful in what he said, but he had to be honest with her. "Do you trust God?" Ironic, he thought, maybe he should take his own advice.

Rylee looked at him. "Well, of course!"

"Then show Him you trust Him. Pray about this and do what God tells you is right. As far as what I think, I understand your hesitancy, but . . . I think you should arrange a chance meeting."

"David, are you sure?" Rylee didn't want that to be his answer.

"Yes, and I'll explain why. You can do as you want. This is just my opinion. Someday, Tyler will want to know his father. It would be better if you didn't hide him. Otherwise, he might not understand. You don't have to formally introduce the two; just casually introduce him as a friend from high school."

As she spoke to David, she put her hand on his arm, "All right. I'll pray about it and let you know what I decide. Thank you for your insight and for being a good friend."

Tyler walked up about that time, "Are you through yet? We want ice cream, please."

"Ice cream coming right up. I have chocolate, vanilla, and cookie dough. Which would you all prefer?" Anything to change the subject, thought Rylee.

"Two vanillas and one cookie dough, please."

David had walked into the living room. "All right, girls, after ice cream, we need to head home. We need to make sure all is ready for school tomorrow."

"Ah, Dad," the girls chimed as they watched Funniest Home Videos.

Laughing, he said, "Enough of that. We've been in Rylee's hair long enough. Be sure and thank Rylee and Tyler for the meal."

The girls finished eating ice cream, they packed up, and left for home. David wanted to meet this guy that was Tyler's father. He wasn't someone he would worry about, but had this guy changed, or was he going to make trouble for the Abrams family? He'd be sure to find out. David's drive home was full of questions. What if he could go with them to accidentally run into this Clint guy? What if this guy was up to something? What if he was getting too involved with Rylee and Tyler?

The next morning, David called Rylee and asked her about going with her. "Rylee, I've been giving it some thought, and would it be all right if I come with you and meet this Clint guy also?"

"Oh, David, I don't know. I want this to be casual, and you wouldn't normally go shopping with me. If you want to be there, that's all right, but please don't arrive with Tyler and me."

"I can understand how that might be awkward. Just let me know where and what time, and I'll find my way. Just playing it safe."

"Thank you, for worrying about me, I suppose. I've been on my own a long time; I'm sure I can handle Clint just fine."

David thought about Rylee all morning, hoping she would call him with some information on when she planned to meet this Clint. He never heard from her, but he kept praying Rylee would call him as soon as she knew anything.

David was busy with the horses when his phone rang. He had left his phone on the desk in the office, so he never heard it. After checking on the number one stud in the group, he walked back into his office and saw that Rylee had called.

Returning her call, he said, "Rylee, it's David. Sorry I missed your call."

"David, I spoke with Clint, and we're going to meet Thursday afternoon at the Waterstown Food Court on the square. Probably around five. I'll see you there if you still want to do that."

"Thanks for calling, Rylee. I wasn't sure you would let me be around."

Relieved that Rylee had called, David made arrangements to leave work a little early so he and the girls could eat at the Downtown Food Court on Thursday. They would be excited. He never took them anywhere on a school night, and this would be a welcome treat. He hoped all would work out according to God's plan.

Six

Rylee prayed for guidance. David was right. Tyler at least needed to meet him whether he knew who he was or not. Thursday couldn't come quick enough. Tyler was excited to go to the food court. It had games and a movie theatre, so he had some ideas in mind. Rylee hated to tell him that they were eating, and that was it! Kids could always come up with something other than what they were supposed to be doing.

Work was busy, Rylee was back in the classroom. The last time she talked about hygiene, this talk was about peer pressure. Rylee and the counselor were teaming up to help all the grades to understand what it meant and hopefully not buy into peer pressure. She worried about the lives of all the children. Rylee brought up bullying and what the children should do.

"Ms. Abrams," one of the sixth-grade students called on her as they raised their hands. "Ms. Abrams, if someone is talking dirty about you on social media, what can they do?"

"I know it's difficult, but the first thing is to tell your parents, then tell the school counselor or myself. It would be best if you didn't face this alone. You are all good kids, and we want you to grow up happy and healthy." When bullying happened to kids, it made Rylee especially upset.

Thursday came to an end, and Rylee had about five students signed up for a one-on-one to talk about bullying. As she left the middle school to pick up Tyler, she remembered where she was headed this evening. Her stomach was doing flip-flops. Rylee was nervous, and she hated it. After they ran home and Rylee changed clothes, she put on makeup and wanted to make herself presentable. She wanted to make a good impression after all these years, then they would head downtown.

∞ ∞ ∞

Clint was ready to meet his kid. He couldn't believe that he didn't have any rights to this boy. He wanted to go to court to get his rights but didn't know if that was the best thing to do. He would like to be a part of Tyler's life, but he wasn't sure if he was ready for the responsibility. Rylee didn't put his name on the birth certificate, and it irritated him. It just read "unknown." He must be on his best behavior; he wanted her to trust him. Clint was trying to straighten his life out. It was time to clean up and get to the Waterstown Food Court.

∞ ∞ ∞

The food court was not busy when David and the girls arrived. He didn't see Rylee anywhere, so he took the girls to the arcade, and they played a game or two. Checking to see if anyone had arrived, he saw Tyler making his way to the arcade with Rylee. Behind her was a tall-hefty football type. David wondered if that was Clint.

"Rylee, what are you and Tyler doing? I didn't think we would see you here. I told the girls we'd play and then eat. When you finish, come and join us, all right?"

"We'll see. Tyler has this one game he wants to play. I have no idea what it is, but he insisted we do it first!" Rylee laughed at Tyler and his 'oh, mom' look. "What was the name of the game, Tyler?"

"It's a dancing game. You follow the colored blocks. I see it on television all the time." Tyler tried to look for it but couldn't find it. "I guess they don't have one." Disappointed he asked, "Can we go eat now?"

David asked, "Would you all like to join us for dinner? Not quite up to the standard of Sunday but filling."

Rylee looked at Tyler. "Do you want to eat with David and the girls?"

"Sure." Tyler was smiling broadly.

"Lead us to your choice!" It happened to be the same place Tyler and Rylee headed, Chick-fil-A, Tyler's favorite!

As they walked David asked her about the football type in the background, "Is that him, you know, Clint?"

Rylee just nodded her head.

They all got what they wanted then headed to a large table set up by the restaurant. Sitting down, it only took Rylee and David three trips to bring napkins and sauce. Finally getting settled, Rylee saw Clint walking up. She so dreaded this encounter.

"Hey, Rylee . . ." Clint was extra cheerful. "Rylee Abrams?" Stopping next to her and Tyler's seats. "Clint Owens from high school. I can't believe it's you. I haven't seen you since school!"

Rylee stood up. "Hello, Clint. I didn't realize you were living around here."

"I don't; I'm just working in the area and came down for a quick meal."

"Well, it's nice to see you. Oh, let me introduce you to my son, Tyler Abrams. Tyler say hello to Mr. Owens."

Tyler didn't miss a beat. "Hello."

David stood up about that time. "Hello, I'm David Hunt. It's nice to meet you, Mr. Owens."

Clint recognized a man claiming his territory. He wondered if Rylee had shared his information with him.

"What have you been doing since graduation?"

"I went back to school, and now I'm a nurse at the middle school in town. How about you, Clint?"

"Construction has been my job since I can remember." Clint was nervous and wanted to cut this short. "It was nice seeing you. Maybe we'll run into each other again." Clint said, turning and walking off.

Tyler spoke up as soon as Clint left. "Who was that man, Mommy? He had blond, curly hair like mine." He turned back around and started talking with the girls again.

Rylee was quiet after that. Now, what would he want? Maybe

she needed to call her lawyer and see what she could expect. Tyler was her son. In the past, Clint wasn't a good man, and she wondered if he had changed. She still didn't want him around Tyler, too much history.

"Rylee . . . Rylee . . . are you all right?" David was trying to get her attention without the kids knowing.

"I'm fine. Clint wants more. I'm calling my lawyer tomorrow and making an appointment. I won't give an inch. I remember he doesn't like to lose." Rylee tried not to be fearful.

David thought he understood. He didn't know what he would do if someone tried to take his girls. Tyler was a good young man.

"Are you finished eating, Tyler?"

"Almost, Mommy. Why are you in such a hurry?"

"I'm sorry, I just know you have homework, and I want time to read you another chapter in your book by Ted Dekker."

"Oh, I can't wait! I'll hurry." Tyler began wolfing his food down.

"Slow down. We're not in that big of a hurry." Rylee laughed at Tyler as he quickly got ready to go home. He loved Ted Dekker's books. They had been reading the Dream Traveler's Quest, and they were on book two. Tyler was a typical boy, loved adventure, and the characters in the book were seeking truth which Tyler's Bible study class was also discussing.

Clint thought as he walked away, he's a fine boy. I sure would like to know him better. Clint drove back to the hotel where he was staying. He knew to bide his time or he would lose out completely. He wondered who the guy was at the table . . . Dennis or Dale. . . he didn't remember his name.

Walking into his hotel room, he picked up the phone and dialed her number.

"Hello." Rylee knew who was calling.

"Hey, what did Tyler say when I left?" Clint blurted out, surprised, she had answered the phone.

"Clint, he didn't say anything. He was more interested in his chicken. Give me a few days, and I'll get back to you." Rylee was upset he had called. She had called her lawyer, a personal friend, and planned on talking with her on Monday. "I'll call you one day next week, okay. Bye."

"Who was that, Mommy?"

"Just a friend. No worries. Let's get to sleep. School tomorrow — remember?"

Rylee tossed and turned for several hours before she fell into a fitful sleep. Nightmares of a strange man taking Tyler was the re-occurring dream that night. When she woke Friday morning, she was tired and cranky. Wishing she could stay home, she included Clint in her morning prayers as she knew he needed Jesus.

Friday was a long, tedious day. It matched Rylee's mood. She had barked at Tyler that morning, and he had left in tears as they drove to school. Hugging him as he got out of the car, he just looked at her.

"I'm sorry, Tyler. Mommy didn't sleep too well last night, but I shouldn't take my bad mood out on you! I love you, buddy." She hated herself at that moment.

"It's all right, Mommy. I know you've been upset since that person came by our table. It will be okay. Jesus has your back. That's what my Sunday School teacher tells me." Jumping out of the car, he waved goodbye and ran to his teacher.

Tears streamed down Rylee's cheeks as she thought about what Tyler had said. Jesus has your back. Even Tyler knew what had upset her, and he was right. She couldn't let him figure all this out before she wanted him to.

Later that morning, Rylee found someone had placed flowers on her desk. She looked for a card, but there wasn't one. Walking into the office, she asked Lyndzey if she knew who had brought them.

"I'll call the florists to find out." It was a small community. There were only two florists, and it wouldn't be hard.

That afternoon Lyndzey came into Rylee's office, "I called the florists, and David Hunt had picked up a small vase of assorted flowers. She said he had a card that he was going to add. Did you look around for it?"

"No, not really, but thank you. I feel much better now." Looking around the desk and on the floor, she still didn't find a card. Oh well, It will show up.

∞∞∞

David stopped by the florist for some cheer-me-up flowers for Rylee. He planned to take them to her that morning, but he couldn't find his card when he arrived at school for drop-off, so he decided to wait until later and went on his way to work.

Running late, as usual, Rylee had already left when he collected Marcie from school, so he and the girls drove by the Abram's house. As David walked to the door, Rylee met him on the porch.

"I can't believe you have brought flowers twice today. You didn't need to." Rylee watched him as he walked to the porch, his face became puzzled, and Rylee knew the flowers at school were from someone else.

"What other flowers? I came to deliver these, but I couldn't find the card when I got to school." David watched Rylee turn and walk back into the house.

∞∞∞

Shaken, that's how she felt, like the world had just shaken her very foundation. Flowers? Did he think she would fall for that? But of course, he did.

David walked inside. "You are white as a sheet. What happened?"

"I got flowers today at work. No card. Lyndzey called the florist, and he gave your name, so I assumed you sent them."

"And you just found out I didn't!"

"Correct."

"I'm so sorry. Have you called your lawyer?" David was worried about Rylee. He hoped her lawyer could figure all this out. "Do you want me to leave?"

"Not really. I was just stunned. What did you think of Clint?"

"I thought he was a big guy and seemed nice. I met him for three seconds. No way to judge someone?"

"David, you are so good for me. You calm me down and make me think. I should listen to you. As far as I know, Clint could have changed. I'll go to see the lawyer and be more cautious. I promise."

David laughed. "I don't have any better insight than you. Don't depend on my judgment."

"Would you like to stay for supper?"

"Not tonight. The girls have riding lessons tonight at the arena, and I promised to read before bedtime. Thank you, though." David turned and walked to the door.

"David, thank you for being a good friend." Rylee enjoyed his company, she liked the way he looked at her, and he always smelled like a fresh breeze. Both of them needed a loving relationship but we're treading carefully.

"Have a nice weekend. We'll see you at church." David left slowly, glad they would see each other again soon.

Rylee smiled, "Bye."

Yep, she needed to be careful, of what she wasn't sure. David had a good chance of catching her and that would be all right, but she wasn't sure she was ready.

Seven

Rylee walked into Ms. Ailene Fowler's office around ten on Monday morning. Her appointment wasn't until ten-thirty, but she needed some time to compose herself. David had called to tell her he was praying, which made her feel supported.

Rachel, Ms. Fowler's secretary, was a friend of Rylee's. She had met both, Ailene and her secretary, at Bible Study on Wednesday night. After that, they began going out for coffee, and she had spilled her life to Ailene. When she finished talking, Ailene told her if she needed anything, just give her a call. Now she did, so here she was.

Ailene reached out to shake Rylee's hand, "Hey, Rylee, come in and sit down. So you've encountered a slight problem — I assume."

"Well, I don't want it to become a problem!" She said, laughing.

"Gotcha. So tell me why you've come to see me today." Ailene was pretty sure she knew, but she wanted to hear Rylee describe the problem.

"Clint Owens is back." Rylee knew that wasn't enough, but it gave her a starting point. "I know him well, and he will start small, and then it will escalate into full war. I'm sure he'll want visiting rights and then full custody. I don't want him to have anything, but I realize that might not happen."

"All right, let me get some particulars, then I'll do a little checking into his lifestyle before we do something to make him angry. How does that sound?"

"Just perfect. You're right. Let's not tick him off too soon." Rylee laughed nervously.

Ailene began, "What has your relationship been with Clint in the past five years?

"Nonexistent, really. I didn't know where he was, and I didn't seek him out." Rylee replied.

"Why do you think Clint is surfacing now?"

"He said he saw my picture in the local paper and that's when he found out I had given birth to a boy. He says he is in town working and wanted to meet Tyler."

"Okay, please don't be in contact with him until I know how we are going to precede. We don't need any issues for either party. I'll get back with you as soon as I know something."

Rylee hugged her friend, "Thank you so much."

Leaving the office, Rylee headed back to school. She had classes she needed to get to, and this meeting went a little longer than expected. The students welcomed her to the classroom with a big round of applause. Rylee smiled. They could be so wonderful.

"We missed you, Ms. Abrams."

"Where were you, Ms. Abrams?"

"Are we going to talk more about bullies?"

Rylee smiled at each one of the children. "We'll pick up where we left off. We talked about being respectful. You gave some excellent answers. Dillon, can you recall any of the suggestions?"

Dillon gave three great answers, and then everyone wanted to answer. By the time they finished, it was the end of class.

It was rewarding for Rylee to help the students with these issues and the teachers appreciated the extra prep time. Once her instruction was over, Rylee went back to her office and began planning for the following health subject for the classrooms.

The weekend was slow in coming. Rylee had made no plans, but she and Tyler headed to the library. Saturday at the library was a zoo. Every child from every school magically appeared for the free programs. Tyler liked to look at books and check one or two out. But wasn't as excited about playing the games with everyone.

Rylee sat down in the children's section, and Tyler went on a hunt. She was searching her phone as Tyler ran around. Looking up to find where her son had gone, she saw a familiar face staring at her — David.

"Hi, what's up?" David had no idea she came to the library on Saturday mornings.

"Gosh, hello, David. I didn't expect to see you here." As Rylee stood up, David reached out his hand to help, accidentally pulling her into him. Rylee stepped back and smiled. "Tyler and I come here once a month to check out books. What are you all doing?"

A little flustered he replied, "We've never been. I thought Susie might enjoy it. Marcie thinks she's too old."

"David, most middle school kids think they are too old for everything." She laughed. "I hope Susie enjoys it; there are a lot of good books and games here. It's nice to see you." Looking towards Tyler, she said, "I think Tyler may have found his books. So we are wrapping things up here. You and the girls have fun." Rylee smiled at David and gave the girls a hug.

"Have a great day, Rylee. Hey, Tyler, what did you find?" David called to Tyler who held up two books.

"Bye." Rylee and Tyler were walking up to the checkout desk.

"Mommy, why didn't we talk to Susie? I like Susie." Tyler was confused.

"I'm sorry, Tyler, I'm tired and didn't feel like having a long conversation. We can go back," she replied turning around to return.

David walked up behind them. "It's all right, Tyler. We all get worn out sometimes. I'll come by and pick you up sometime this weekend, and you can go riding with the girls while Mommy unwinds."

"Can I, Mommy, can I?" Tyler was excited.

"Sounds good, kiddo. You run to the car, and I'll make arrangements with David, okay."

"Okay, I'll go read my book." Tyler was so excited.

"I appreciate you inviting Tyler. He will love it, but check with me first next time." Rylee smiled. "I don't want him to think he doesn't have to check with me first. You know, David, I am so grateful for the time you have spent with Tyler. He loves you, and I want him to have a role model to look up too. Thank you."

"You're right. I should have asked you first. I love him, too, in fact I think both of you are very special." As David walked off, he turned to Rylee. "How about after church? Will that be okay?"

S.B. ROTH

"That's great. Maybe I can take Marcie and we could do a little shopping." Rylee hadn't forgotten about Marcie's request.

∞∞∞

David was kicking himself all the way home. He knew life for Rylee was a little rough right now. He should be looking for positive ways to make her life easier, not butting in where he didn't need to.

He'd talk with her after church on Sunday about picking Tyler up to go riding. Tyler would be a good horseback rider. David would pair him with a small chestnut horse that very slow due to age. He just needed to learn how to address the horse, lead the horse, and then they'd work on brushing him down. Depending on how Tyler did would determine if he even sat on the horse this time. The girls were excited, and he figured Tyler would be too. Now they needed the weather to cooperate. Fall storms had been popping up off and on for a few days.

Rylee found Tyler in his room and filled him in on the plans. Rylee laughed when he started jumping around and acting like a horse.

Sunday dawned bright and beautiful, so Tyler filled his backpack with what he would need to go horseback riding and took it to church with him. As they entered the building, he saw David and the girls and ran to them. "Mommy, can we sit with the girls?"

"If they don't mind, then I don't mind, Tyler," she said, laughing at his exuberance. "Good morning, Hunt family. Isn't it great to be in God's house again?"

David leaned over and whispered in Rylee's ear, "Did you notice who was sitting in the back pew on the other side of the sanctuary? Take a look."

Rylee began to turn slowly and look at the people around them. She could see a curly, blond headed man sitting on the other side of the church about four pews behind them. Clint. Every instinct inside her wanted to get up and run, but the fact that Tyler

44

reminded her that Jesus had her back and Clint was in church made her reevaluate her thoughts. It wasn't long before the Praise Team began to sing one of her favorite songs by Kari Jobe and Cody Carnes, The Blessing. The entire congregation stood and sang with them, and God comforted her.

Eight

Rylee left church lonely. She was determined not to go with Tyler. It was time he did a few things without her. Besides she and Marcie were going girl shopping. Marcie hopped in the car with Rylee.

"I bet this is different than having Tyler around. Thank you for taking me."

"Well, I didn't want you to think I had forgotten your request!" Rylee smiled at Marcie.

Rylee and Marcie drove to the closest big town and spent a little girl time getting the necessary garments for Marcie.

It was different going home to an empty house with no Tyler, but she wanted to use this time to get a few things done for the week. Marcie had brought a book she was reading and sat down in the living room to read while Rylee was busy. Occasionally Marcie would pop in and ask if she could help, but for the most part Rylee had time to think. She packed the basics for their lunches for a week, then she put a roast on to cook and fried a chicken. Having this meat prepped for their lunches was such a nice feeling. Plus, they could eat it at night too. By the time she finished, it was about time for Tyler to be home. She couldn't wait to hear about the fantastic time he had.

Hearing her phone ring in the other room, she hurried to get it. Looking at the caller, she saw it was David, "Hello, David. Is everything all right?"

"Of course, we had a great time. I wanted you to know that we will be stopping for ice cream before I bring Tyler home. Is that okay?"

"That's fine. Bring Marcie something. She's been a doll. Thank you for calling." Rylee ended the call and looked for Tyler's dirty clothes to put in the washer. That boy could get so much dirt on his clothes it was amazing there was any left outside. Such is the luck of having a boy! But she wouldn't trade him for the world. She picked up her few things, plus the towels, and into the washer they went. It was about four-thirty, and she was ready for a break.

Marcie had fallen asleep on the couch while reading, so Rylee woke her for some lemonade and they sat out on the porch waiting on Tyler to arrive with David. As Marcie sat she sang several songs from church to herself. Rylee loved to hear her. She let her mind wander back over her meeting with Clint and realized she was the one blowing things out of proportion. Clint might have changed. She didn't know. She had to give him a chance. Not because of her, but because Rylee knew if Tyler didn't have a father around, he would begin to question her a lot over the next ten years. She wanted him to have answers.

Marcie had been watching Rylee as she struggled within her mind, "Rylee, what are you thinking about? You seem upset."

"Not really upset, Marcie. Just sometimes life heads in a direction you're not sure about. Luckily I have you to set me straight!" she said, smiling at the cute teenager sitting next to her.

It wasn't long until David and Susie were letting Tyler out of the car. Marcie picked up her package and ran to the car. Everyone waved goodbye as Tyler began running to the porch.

"Bye Rylee, thank you, I love you." Marcie smiled all the way to the car.

"Mommy, I had so much fun. Can I do it again next week? You should see the horse I was riding. I learned to walk him, and then we brushed him, then I put the saddle on him."

"Slow down, Tyler. So you got to get on him today and ride?"

"Well, David sat me on the horse and led me a little way, but no, I didn't get to do it by myself. But next week!"

"We shall see about next week. Let's get in the house. You need a bath then to clean your room while I get supper ready." Rylee could smell the horse coming off of Tyler as soon as he hit the porch.

"Ah, Mommy. Do I have to take a bath?" Tyler hated soap and

water.

"Yes, sir, you most certainly do. Now go."

Tyler just looked at his mother and went to the bathroom. While he was bathing, she put their meal together, hoping he would eat after having ice cream.

She needed to get ahead of this mood she'd been in. She thought the world of David and his girls. In fact, she really like him, but she had been too moody for anyone to be around lately.

∞∞∞

The following day was Monday, and Tyler acted like he never went to school on Mondays. Cranky, lazy, and not wanting to get dressed.

"Okay, young man. If you aren't ready by the time I come back in here, you will not—I repeat—not, go horseback riding next week. Understood?"

Rylee was over his attitude.

Tyler just sat there as she left the room. The minute she was out of sight, he hurriedly put on his clothes and then sat on the couch in the living room. When Rylee walked back into his room a few minutes later, he was gone.

"So you didn't have any trouble getting dressed when I threatened to take away something that you like. I don't want to have that happen again, Tyler, or you will not be seeing a horse for the entire school year. If you can't be ready for school, then you can't plan afterschool or weekend activities."

"Yes, ma'am." Tyler knew he was wrong. He should have done it at the start. They were studying the Ten Commandments in Bible study, Honor your father and mother . . . since his mother was all he had, he better honor her even more.

Riding to school, Tyler began, "Mommy, I'm sorry. I was so tired. That made me bad, I guess. I will honor you as the verse tells me to."

"The only person to blame is yourself, sweetheart, but sometimes we do things that we absolutely know are wrong, but we still do them. You'll get better. I will always love you whatever you choose to do." Rylee said, wanting to reassure Tyler.

Arriving at school, Tyler jumped out of the car, and Rylee headed to the middle school. She had a full day in the classrooms teaching drug awareness. Most of the seventh and eighth-grade classes had finished the course, but now it was the sixth graders chance to hear her favorite unit. She would be teaching in the science classrooms all week.

She saw Marcie sitting with a seventh-grade boy during lunch duty, so she sauntered over to be a little nosey. "Hey, Marcie, who's your friend?"

Marcie turned seven shades of red, "This is Joel. We have the same math class, and he needs some help, so we're talking about math." Marcie was embarrassed to be caught talking to a boy. She hadn't even told her daddy about him.

"That's good. You two have fun, learn a lot." Rylee headed away from the table. She should apologize to Marcie. She didn't mean to upset her in any way.

After school, she found Marcie and took her into her office. "I'm sorry, Marcie. I didn't mean to put you on the spot at lunch—just a bad mistake on my part. I won't say anything to your dad. That's your business."

"Thank you, Ms. Abrams. My dad would freak out. He thinks I'm a little baby and that I think boys have cooties! We are just good friends, and he is in my math class, and I am helping him."

"No problem, sweetheart. That's very nice of you."

Looking out the office window, she saw David and Susie enter with Tyler. David had begun to pick up Susie and Tyler and then bring Tyler to the middle school when he picked up Marcie. It worked out well for both of them.

Tyler came running, and David walked into the office. "Hey, Marcie, are you ready? Girls run get in the car, please. Rylee, do you have any plans this evening?" Taking Rylee's hand he said, "Would you like to get some ice cream after supper tonight? I could drop by and we could run the kids up to the Sugar and Sweet for an hour."

"That's sounds nice, David. I'd love to. Just call when you're on your way. Thanks for bringing Tyler."

"You're welcome. I'll see you later." Squeezing her hand a little, he let go, turned, and left the building.

Rylee just stood there looking at her hand. His touch had felt right.

"Mommy, let's go." Tyler was ready to go home.

∞∞∞

As Rylee pulled into the driveway, her phone rang several times. She let it go to voicemail and then took a look — a message from Clint. Now, what does he want? she thought.

Listening to her voicemail she found out, "Rylee, this is Clint. I just was wondering if we could work something out so I could see Tyler again? I'm finishing my job in Waterstown, and I'd like to get to know him a little better before I move on. Please call me at this number."

Well, Clint is leaving soon. Rylee thought the more they saw each other, the worse it would be, but maybe it was time to tell Tyler about his father. First, she wanted to meet with Clint alone and discuss what he could and could not say. If Clint could be reasonable, then she could too.

She wanted to call David, but she'd see him tonight. Until then, she'd do this on her own. Calling Clint was not easy, but she called him anyway.

"Clint, this is Rylee. Let's meet first and hammer out a few things before we bring Tyler into the meeting." Rylee was shaking.

Clint couldn't believe she called him back. "That's fine. Just when and where?"

"Let me get a babysitter, and I'll call you back. One evening this week would be best for me. We can go to the Frosty Cream for burgers. Any day but Wednesday." Rylee said goodbye and hung up.

Rylee called several people for babysitting and found no one.

Ugh! She thought. I suppose I'll call David.

"Hello," David said, "you're not backing out of ice cream tonight?"

Laughing a little, Rylee continued, "No, but what are you doing around five-thirty Thursday evening?"

"Not a thing that I have scheduled. What are you thinking?" David was hoping they might get together.

"Well, I have a meeting at six and need someone to watch Tyler for about an hour and a half. Think you and the girls could come over for a little while? I tried everyone else."

"Of course, we can. What do you have going on? Or is it none of my business?" David chuckled.

"I need to meet with Clint to discuss Tyler, and I don't want Tyler there."

"Maybe I need to be there." David didn't like her going to see Clint without him.

"I'll be fine. We're going to meet at the Frosty Cream for hamburgers. We'll be fine."

Finally, David agreed to watch Tyler, and Rylee called Clint back and set up the meeting. Now, she thought, this needs a whole lot of prayer.

Nine

Rylee found a table in the back corner of the Frosty Cream, so they'd be left alone. She had been working on a list of things Clint had to agree on before she would tell Tyler about his father and allow them to meet. First, he had never been there for Tyler, so don't talk about custody rights. Clint had no rights as far as she was concerned. Second, he was never to blindside her by coming to the house without a phone call first.

She knew David was unhappy about this meeting. He had held her hand and pleaded with her to let him go with her.

"Rylee, don't do this without someone else there. You don't know where this might be headed. If he abused you once, he might hit out at you again." David held tightly to her hand.

"David, I'll be all right. I promise I won't back him into a corner. Trust me. Keeping Tyler is the best thing you can do for me right now."

David had pulled her closer to him and hugged her tightly. "I can't lose you, Rylee. I feel like you are saving me, and I need to save you. Please be careful."

"I'll be careful, David. I promise."

Tyler was happy to have his friends over but curious where Rylee was going. When he asked her, she simply told him she had an appointment and to mind David while she was out.

As Rylee sat in the booth, she watched as an old Ford truck pulled up in front of the Frosty Cream. Clint got out and came lumbering into the building. He was a big guy and used to move pretty fast, but that wasn't happening tonight. As he entered, Rylee waved from the back table, and he walked over.

"Rylee," he said, leaning over with an outstretched hand, "nice to see you again."

"Hello, Clint. Let's order first, then we can talk." The waitress took their order and then Rylee continued. "Well, here we are about six years later. Let's get this settled. I know you're not the same person. Why don't you tell me who you are and where you've been?" Rylee wasn't cutting him any slack. She wanted some answers before she could make a sound decision.

"Well, I got married, and then spent some time in jail for abuse. Once I got out, I began attending a counseling program for people with abuse or anger problems. I graduated from the program, and there have been no abuse or anger problems since then. I learned my lesson, Rylee, and I'm glad that I've grown up."

"I'm happy for you, Clint, but that doesn't change how I feel about you getting to know Tyler."

The waitress brought their hamburgers and sodas. They both took a bite or two before Rylee continued. "Good hamburger. You know, Clint, Tyler is my world, and he is going to be hurt to know that you were around all this time but never came to see him. So why now?" Rylee couldn't afford to give him an inch. She was honest, if nothing else.

"That wasn't all my fault. You never contacted me." Clint began to put up that shield again.

"Then whose fault was it, Clint? I left for fear of my life. You didn't come to the hospital. You didn't try to find Tyler or me. You just happened to find us now. I don't believe you. Where have you been? What do you do for work? Do you have a girlfriend?"

Clint stayed quiet for a long time, taking a few bites of his burger. Rylee was right, he thought. He couldn't blame anyone but himself. If he wasn't careful, he would be back in the same place he was five years ago. "You're right. This is what I've been fighting all my life — it isn't my fault. That's wrong. I know I was to blame for never meeting my son. I've been traveling around with a construction company. I really didn't know where you were until I saw your picture in the newspaper, and that's when I saw I had a son. I haven't had a girlfriend since I got out of prison. I think the classes I went to helped me the most. I want to try to be the man that Tyler deserves for a father. I understand why you are hesitating, but thank you for giving me an opportunity to at least know him now."

Rylee wasn't sure what she wanted to do with all this. She didn't want Clint to tear up Tyler's life, but if they worked it correctly, then maybe it would be okay. They had to work this out for Tyler.

"All right, Clint. Here's what we will do. I will lay the groundwork by telling Tyler all the good things about you. After that settles down, I will suggest that he meets you only if he wants to. It will be completely up to him. When he feels it's okay, then and only then will you be allowed to come to our house. That might take a while. Are you prepared to wait?"

"I can agree with that."

"Then let's pray. Give me your hands."

Clint didn't know what was happening, but he put his hands out, and Rylee grabbed them. "Okay, Lord. Here we are as Tyler's parents, leaving our son in Your hands. When he was born, I gave him to You, and You have brought us to this point. You are Lord over everything. Please guide each of us in words, actions, and what we do. Your will be done. Amen."

Clint felt at peace when Rylee finished. Rylee once again reminded herself that all things are under His control.

They left with an understanding. Rylee would call Clint when she felt Tyler was ready.

Arriving back at her house, David was staring out the front window waiting on her. She laughed as she saw him when she pulled into the driveway. He was at the car before she could turn it off.

"Is everything all right? What took you so long? What did you two decide?" David had been pacing the floor since she left.

"Slow down, David." Rylee smiled at him. "All is fine. We ordered and ate hamburgers, silly. I'll tell you all about it. Sit with me on the porch while the kids are occupied."

"Well, what did he say?"

"He caught me up on the last six years of his life, and we talked a little, then I told him exactly what you and I had discussed. Plus,

Ailene Fowler gave me some good pointers when I saw her last week at her office. It will all work according to Tyler's timeline."

"Phew, I was sweating bullets. I'm so glad you feel confident in this. I know we've only known each other a few months, but you have been a stabilizing force in my life and my girl's life."

"Thank you, David." Rylee thought she might want more that being stable! She laughed to herself

"I wasn't sure I would ever feel like moving on since my wife died, but you've given me hope to look forward to life."

Rylee just looked at David, knowing that he was becoming important to her but not wanting to overstep. "Thank you, David. I would like for you to be with me when I tell Tyler about his father. You can be in the kitchen or outside but somewhere if he needs a man to talk to."

"I would feel privileged to be able to help. Just let me know when." David felt honored.

"I'll call and let you know. I want to approach this carefully. I told Clint we wouldn't talk until Tyler wanted to meet him. So I don't know how long that might be. Clint agreed even though it might be two years from now."

They stood at the same time, and Rylee turned to walk into the house. David put his hands on her shoulders, and they stared into each other's eyes. Moving closer to her, David lowered his head and placed a well-thought-out kiss on her lips. Rylee responded before moving away.

"I'm sorry, David, I didn't mean for that to happen. I know you're still grieving your wife, and I wouldn't want you to think . . ."

"I kissed you, silly. I wanted to kiss you." David was fighting the response to kiss her again and again.

"It was to comfort me, that's all." Rylee was very uncomfortable.

"I wasn't comforting you. If anyone needs comfort, it was me! I want you to be the one to comfort me, too."

"Don't you think we should slow down? I would love to have you in my messy life, but I want you to be sure you're ready. Plus, I have to deal with Tyler."

"Oh, Rylee, I'm ready, more than ready."

Reaching up, she kissed him a second time. Only she initiated this one.

Ten

Clint left the Frosty Cream with a renewed sense of hope. Rylee was going to allow Tyler to know him as his father. It may take some time, but he knew that it would help him release some of the guilt he felt for his actions back then. He wasn't too good at biding his time, but he would work on his patience. Rylee didn't say how long. She did promise to call him, and then she prayed. Boy, things had changed over the last several years.

He had never been very religious, but for some reason, that prayer made him trust her even more. It's too bad we didn't make it back then, he thought. They were different people. Now was the right time.

Arriving at work, Clint saw his boss waving him over.

"Hey, Clint. I need to talk with you." Clint had worked for John Bates for a little over a year, and John was impressed with the young man. Clint had been in charge of framing and roofing for most of his time with the company. He needed a license for plumbing and electricity, but he hadn't done that yet.

"Yes, sir. Did I do something?" Clint was shaking. He knew he had done an excellent job, but he was so used to screwing up. It was normal to think he was in trouble.

"What you've done, young man is a fine job for my company. I can depend on you, and I wanted to let you know that you will be my right-hand man on our next job. I want to train you to be in charge of a project. It will be a while until we start. But I know I can depend on you totally to do the right kind of job." John slapped Clint on the back and then shook his hand. "Does that sound good to you?"

"Oh, yes, sir. Thank you. I'm encouraged. I'm glad I'm doing a good job." Clint wanted to dance a little jig, but he refrained. Wow, he was over the top excited. Just don't screw up, he thought.

∞∞∞

Ranger Middle School was decorated for the Christmas Holidays. The teachers had outdone themselves, and the students were in the swing of things too. In the Deck the Halls contest, each hall had been decked out by a different grade and then judged by the high school art teacher. The eighth grade had won the hall decorating contest (as usual), but in a surprise move the sixth grade had come in second. Each Friday from after Thanksgiving Break until Christmas Break was designated dress up day, and the costumes were to be of the students' favorite Christmas animal, or character, or movie. They were so excited and it made the last three weeks before Christmas wild at the middle school. The middle school talent show was set for December 20th, the last day of school before the holidays. The school was excited.

The choir department was having tryouts for anyone wanting to participate. Marcie had come to Rylee and asked for help with her song she planned to sing. Marcie would come

into Rylee's office after school, and she would work with her on personality and butterflies since Rylee couldn't help with the singing. Tone-deaf was always her excuse. On the other hand, Marcie was gifted musically, and Rylee would be surprised if she didn't win.

David was picking up Tyler for her, and he would wait with Susie and Tyler while Rylee helped Marcie. The relationship between them had been a little awkward after the kiss, but it reverted back into the comfortable stage. Otherwise the only kisses exchanged lately were on the cheek as a greeting or a goodbye. However, both were ready to move forward.

Rylee had decided to talk to Tyler the day after school would be out. This would allow him time to process everything before going back to school. They had spoken so little about a daddy over the years that she honestly wasn't sure how he would react.

She was glad that David would be nearby in case she needed his guidance.

The last Friday before school was out, Marcie came running into her office, sobbing her eyes out.

"I can't do it, Ms. Abrams. I cannot get on stage and sing BY MYSELF. Please help me get out of this. What was I thinking?" Marcie was shaking like a leaf.

"What happened, little one? Why are you so nervous all of a sudden? You know you can sing the pants off a squirrel. There is no need to be nervous." Rylee sat her down in a chair then sat down beside her.

"Jacob Bell, he said . . . he said . . ." sobbing her eyes out, "only a crazy person would sing by themselves. He didn't think I could do it. He just went on and on about Abby being the best singer in the ENTIRE school."

Hug, hold, and hush was the best advice she had been given many years ago. If someone is hurting, you just have to wait until they could go on. It was true for everyone, even for a seventh-grader, and sure enough, Marcie stopped sobbing.

After thinking a few minutes, Marcie continued, "How would Jacob know? He's never heard either one of us sing. Besides, I won the District Choir contest, and Abby didn't even place. She's good but not MY good!"

Rylee cracked up, "Let's not let our pride get the best of us. You are both good. One of you will probably win the contest. It's not about winning. It's more about participating and being involved in school activities."

Marcie and Rylee sat and talked for a few minutes about believing what everyone is saying, and the best thing you can do is speak to the person calmly. Being in middle school had been hard for Rylee, and she knew Marcie would have a few bad times, too.

"Let me write you a pass back to class. Don't pay any attention to what people are saying. Build that confidence by knowing that you will do the best you can in the talent show whether you win or not."

"You're right, Ms. Abrams. Thank you," she said, hugging

Rylee, then turning and hurrying back to class. Marcie would be all right.

Rylee called David to let him be aware of Marcie's feelings and pump her up a little. She also suggested he take time to be at the talent show on the twentieth. "Why don't you surprise Marcie at the talent show? If she asks if you're coming, tell her you'll try. Then show up! She will be so excited."

"Great plan, Rylee. I'll put that in my schedule. What are you all doing on Christmas Eve? We have a great party in the barn out here. Santa brings goodies, there's dancing, and lots of food. There is even a silent auction to raise money for St. Jude's Hospital in Memphis. I'd love for you and Tyler to attend."

"We usually go to the candlelight service at the church and then go home and read the Christmas story in Luke, but we could stop by for a little while. What time does it begin?"

"Usually around four, and then food is served at five. I'll pick you up and then we can go to the candlelight service later. Does that sound all right?"

"Oh I think that would be perfect! We would love to join you and the girls!" Rylee thought it sounded like fun, and she knew Tyler would enjoy it.

David thought a minute before he asked, "Have you decided when you're going to talk to Tyler about Clint?"

Rylee wished they weren't on the phone, it was easier to see what David was thinking in person, but she answered anyway. "I told Clint I would talk with Tyler a few days after school was out, before the holiday ended, and I will. I'm thinking sometime after church this Sunday. Right now, I have to get back to work. Bye." Hanging up, she began looking through student charts again, checking shot records for eighth graders going into high school at the end of the year. Tedious. The high school required a copy of the records by April, and it took a while to go through all the charts.

That evening she opened up the computer and began mapping out a vacation for Tyler and her for the coming summer. She wanted him to see some of the National Parks and planned to go to the Grand Canyon this summer. It was a surprise for his birthday in April. He'd be so excited.

Sunday came, and Tyler and Rylee headed to church. As usual, the Hunt family was already there and greeted them when they arrived. The kids ran to the usual place they sat, and David and Rylee talked as they headed to the pew, talking with several people as they walked. It wasn't until Rylee turned to enter the bench that she saw Clint sitting on the back row of the section. He gave a little wave which she returned before she sat down.

"David," she wanted him to be aware, "don't turn around, but Clint is sitting on the back pew."

David had a strong urge to stand, turn, and glare, but he didn't, "What's he doing here?"

"Well, I hope it means he's attempting to get right with God. Otherwise, I don't care. I'm just glad he came." Rylee was glad they had prayed at the end of their meeting. The best thing for Clint would be to see Jesus and what He could do for Clint's life.

The praise team outdid themselves, and the preacher was on fire. He spoke of the birth of Christ, and the hardships that Christ endured, and yet from those hardships came the Savior of the world. As they left, Rylee tried to find Clint and thank him for coming, but he was nowhere to be found. She needed to sit down today and tell Tyler about his birth and biological father, minus the rough stuff. But would she be able to? She was dreading it since she wasn't sure his reaction. Maybe she'd wait until after Christmas.

But first, they were headed to lunch at the Bronco Diner. It had been a good day.

Eleven

The Ranger Middle School Talent Show was terrific. So many kids put together karaoke productions that were so funny, and one group of boys did a football skit while another group did a parody on a Beach Boys song. Rylee and David were glad they didn't have to judge the contest. In the end, three performances were on top: Marcie Hunt – Voice; Dean Lowe – Musical Instrument; The Beach Boy Group - Parody. Everyone had a great time. There were sounds of great joy when the bell rang, and the students left until the fifth of January.

Walking out of the building, Rylee felt a sense of relief that she and Tyler could relax for the next few days. Christmas Eve was four days away, and she was ready. All the trappings of the holidays were ready, and they had the church service and the party at the ranch. Wanting to talk to Tyler about Clint was going to take place after Christmas. They were so busy, and she didn't want to spoil his Christmas. At that point Tyler would begin to learn about his father. She prayed that he would listen and be happy to know his father was around.

In the past, Rylee had never told Tyler anything about Clint. She had told him a little on Sunday, but that's as far as it had gotten, but now he would learn more. God assured her it would be all right.

The next few days centered on the party at David's barn and the candlelight service at church. The party at the barn was filled with people Rylee had not met before. She spent hours trying to decide what to wear for the party that would also be appropriate for church. Finally, Tyler told her she looked nice and figured that was all she was going to get out of her son. Rylee and Marcie had looked days before through Rylee's closet for something Rylee

could wear to the party, and Marcie had picked out two outfits from which she was to choose. She settled, so to speak, on a light green dress with navy accents. She knew the party was in the barn so she wore flats that she bought for the occasion.

David picked Rylee and Tyler up early, so he could greet his guests when they arrived. When he saw Rylee he couldn't be quiet and whistled his best catcall. Rylee laughed and returned his complement with her own whistle.

"Well, I'd say you look might fine, Mr. Hunt. Do we really have to attend your party?" Raising her eyebrows just a tad.

"I'll bow out early if you're offering to accompany me. This might be a late night. You look absolutely stunning, Rylee." David's heart was beating rapidly.

Suddenly, Tyler chimed in, "Would you two forget this mushy stuff? Are the girls in the car?"

Both Rylee and David laughed and got in the car. They had forgotten Tyler was close by. Rylee had bought David a small gift, a keychain and had the girls names engraved on the front and back, but she was waiting until they were alone to give it to him.

The barn was amazing. White twinkle lights everywhere, colorful blankets thrown over the haybales, plus chairs and tables filled with appetizers placed on them. David spent a lot of his time introducing her and talking with other employees from the ranches. Rylee and David danced to the live music once or twice.

Rylee commented, "You smell absolutely delicious Mr. Hunt. Is your cologne new?"

"I think it's one the girls gave me last Christmas, pretty good if you like it. You know that I think you're beautiful. But tonight with the lights twinkling and the music playing, I can't describe how lovely you are. You always smell delicious, and you always look fabulous, Rylee." He pulled her closer to him and leaned down to place a light feather kiss on her neck.

Rylee had chills go through her like never before, "Oh dear." Shivering a little. "It looks like Santa has arrived."

There was a special event for the children, Santa Claus made a quick appearance before leaving to deliver presents to good little girls and boys. David tried to get alone with Rylee but it wasn't happening at this party. After that last dance, he wanted more, but time was running out and they would need to leave. He had bought Rylee a charm bracelet for Christmas. It had two charms on it, one had Tyler written on it and his birthdate, the other was a small heart in the middle of Texas, placed about where Waterstown was located. He prayed she liked it.

About seven o'clock, David, Rylee and the children left for the candlelight service. Christmas hymns were sung and the preacher shared the story of Jesus' birth from Luke. After the service, the worshipers stood outside the church and sang hymns to those passing by. The children's church had set up a live nativity scene, and many drove by to hear the music and see what the children had done.

The party at the ranch had been extra special for Rylee. Rylee asked David to drop them off at home after the church service. They needed to put cookies out for Santa and place baby Jesus in the manger scene. As Rylee prepared to get out of the car, David pulled her back and gave her a kiss and handed her a present. Opening the small box, she found the charm bracelet he had bought for her with the two charms.

"Oh, I love it. Thank you so much." Leaning over she kissed him generously. "Merry Christmas, David."

"I think we can do better than that." Pulling her close, he said, "Merry Christmas, Rylee."He took her in his arms and kissed her sweetly but with passion.

Wow, thought Rylee. "I have a little something for you too." She handed him his present.

David opened and found the key ring with the girls' names engraved on it. "Thank you, it's perfect, Rylee. It's funny we both wanted to remind ourselves of the kids." Kissing her again he thanked her one more time.

Tyler worn out, but still excited, had asked Santa for a train set, and Rylee had bought the best she could afford. He would spend all Christmas Day putting it together. He had always loved trains and said he wanted to be an engineer when he grew up.

Rylee would smile and tell him that sounded like fun.

"Mommy?" Tyler had a question for her.

"Yes, Tyler. What do you need?" Rylee knew he would start in with the same questions.

"How does Santa fly all over the world and deliver all those presents to all the kids? Do you think he's real, Mommy?"

Rylee thought for a few minutes, then began, "Tyler do you believe in miracles? He nodded his head. "If you do, then you shouldn't be concerned with how Santa does what he does. Jesus sends us miracles in all shapes and sizes. Maybe Santa is a miracle that Jesus thinks we need one night a year. It sure makes Christmas fun when we believe in Santa."

"I know, Mommy, but Christmas is really about the birth of Jesus. Does everybody know that?"

"If they don't, Tyler, we should share that news with them. That's the best gift of all. Now it's time to go to bed. Tomorrow is a big day!" Rylee tickled him into the bedroom, and he fell on his bed laughing.

"I love you, Mommy." Tyler hugged her extra tight.

"I love you, Tyler." Rylee hugged him extra tight. "Goodnight!"

It wasn't hard to fall asleep. Rylee and Tyler had both had a busy day. They always prayed for snow on Christmas morning, but that didn't often happen in Texas, and according to the weatherman, it wasn't going to happen this year either.

Tip-toeing through the living room that night. A present was placed under the tree for Tyler Abrams – From Santa.

The next morning Rylee awoke long after sunrise. Stretching her arms and yawning, she thought, it's Christmas Day and she needed to get breakfast going. Hopping out of bed, she couldn't hear Tyler, so she assumed he was still asleep, but she was wrong.

Sitting in the middle of the living room in front of the tree, Tyler was carefully figuring out how to put his new train set together. Rylee grabbed her camera and began taking pictures before he saw she was awake. She rarely got these unaware photos, and she was surprised he hadn't heard her.

"Oh, Mommy, look what Santa brought me!" Tyler was up to his elbows in train parts and train tracks.

"Wow, Tyler. That is just like the one you wanted. You must have been a good boy this year. You'll have to write Santa a big thank you note."

"I know, Mommy. I guess Santa didn't get my other list." His little mouth turned downward.

Rylee stopped and thought a minute. She hadn't seen another list. "What other list, Tyler?"

"The one we did at school and mailed. I asked Santa if he could find my daddy." Tyler kept on putting his train together.

Rylee stood still. Now, why would he ask that? she wondered. "Tyler, why did you ask that?"

"I want to have a daddy like Susie has a daddy. Can we find him, please?"

"I'll tell you what, let's eat a big breakfast, put your train together, and then we can talk about it. How does that sound, Tyler?"

"Just perfect, Mommy."

While Tyler finished his breakfast of pancakes, sausage, and orange juice, Rylee tried to decide what she would do. David invited them to Christmas Day lunch at twelve-thirty at the ranch with him and the girls. She had accepted the invitation and knew they would have to hurry before going.

Putting the dishes in the sink, she had Tyler take a shower, dress, and clean his room, and she would do the same. Then and only then would she answer his questions. They could talk about it as they drove to the ranch. He rushed to the bathroom. She heard the shower and peeked in to make sure he was in it. Tyler was new to showering without her help. He did pretty well, but she always had to clean his ears and wash his hair in the sink.

"Use soap, young man!" she ordered as she closed the door.

"Oh, man, I am Mommy."

She chuckled as she went back to the kitchen and finished cleaning the dishes. Next, she texted David. She didn't want to interrupt his morning with the girls.

Rylee – *Tyler stunned me this morning, asking about Clint. Not sure we should come for lunch today.*

David – *Come anyway. We can talk then.*

Rylee – *All right, see you then. And Merry Christmas!*

Well, she had warned him. Tyler came into the kitchen with a wet, curly head of blond hair. He began playing with his train while she went to shower and change. Trying to decide how to approach the subject, she decided she would ask Tyler what his questions were and then answer them without detail.

Standing in the shower gave her time to relax and once again remind herself that Jesus had it all under control. She just needed to give it back to Him. That was the hard part. Rylee thought she had it under control — wrong.

Once she was dressed and finished putting her wet hair into a ponytail, she walked into the living room to find Tyler unwrapping a present she had never seen before.

"Where did that come from, Tyler?"

"Someone knocked on the door. I looked out the window like you told me, and no one was there. So I opened the door and picked it up."

"You know not to open the door while I'm showering. You're in hot water, young man." What was all this, Rylee thought.

"But Mommy, it has my name on it, and it says, 'From Dad.'"

Twelve

Rylee sat down on the couch. She could not believe that after all their talking, Clint still did something without asking. Now what? Tyler was excited. The train was put aside, and he was playing with the ball and glove that Clint had gotten him.

"Tyler, put that down and come over here."

"But Mommy, it's from my real daddy. Please, can I play? Santa didn't forget."

Rylee was so unsure of herself as a mom. She was getting better, but sometimes she just needed a listening ear. She needed to call David. She and Tyler needed to leave for the ranch in an hour. She'd let Tyler play, and she would call Clint!

Rylee looked at her phone. She knew Clint was expecting she would call. She assumed he hadn't seen Tyler, unless he hid from his car and watched Tyler open the door.

She snuck into her bedroom and made the call.

"Hello, Rylee. I was anticipating your call," Clint's voice exuded confidence.

"Where are you?" she asked with a hint of fury.

"Driving back to my hotel. Is he enjoying the gift?"

"What are you doing? . . . We had an agreement. I thought we were both on the same page. I came into the living room to talk with Tyler, and there it was, you'd done all the talking."

"Hold on. You said you'd get back to me. What does it hurt if he gets a present from me for Christmas?"

"Other than you can't hold to your word. Now I'm not sure I'll be able to trust you again. Goodbye." Rylee ended the call and threw the phone on her bed.

Tyler walked into the bedroom where Rylee was and asked, "Who was that on the phone?"

"Oh, my goodness, you scared me, sneaking up on me like that!" Please Lord, help me. Ignoring his question she said, "Are you ready to go out to the ranch to see the Hunt's?"

"Sure."

"Maybe you can go horseback riding again while we're there. I know you love it, so more lessons will be coming your way."

"Thank you, Mommy."

"Well, I've got to let you grow up sometime, don't I? After all, you have a birthday in April."

Tyler jumped up and down, "Yeah! Maybe my daddy will send me another present. Does he know my birthday, Mommy?"

"You know, Tyler, I don't know if he does. He wasn't around, and he didn't ask." Rylee knew that was harsh, but she needed him to see his "daddy" as he was, not as he seemed to be. "You know when you were born your dad didn't know where I lived. We had parted and didn't see each other anymore. I'm sure it was years before he ever found out about his son. But now that he knows about you, he wants to know you personally, okay?"

"Okay." Tyler turned to grab his ball and glove before they headed to the ranch.

∞∞∞

David was worried about Rylee and Tyler. They were a little late. David knew that she was talking to Tyler about Clint, and maybe they weren't through. Standing at the barn door, he finally saw Rylee's car headed down the drive and was relieved.

"Merry Christmas! I'm so glad you guys were able to make it!" David looked at Rylee and saw she was upset. "Tyler, is that what Santa brought you?" Tyler was throwing the ball in the air and catching it with his glove.

"No, my daddy."

You could have heard a pin drop as David immediately looked at Rylee and saw tears in her eyes.

"Cool. Hey Tyler, the girls are waiting for you at the house.

Why don't you head up there? I've got something to show your mom."

"Okay. Is that all right, Mommy?"

"Of course, sweetheart." As soon as Tyler was out of earshot, Rylee stepped into the barn and collapsed into David's arms.

David held her for a few minutes and allowed her to sob her heart out. He already knew the story. Maybe not the details, but Tyler had told him all he needed to know. Clint had shattered her peace.

"Oh, David, what a morning. I should be celebrating the birth of Christ, and instead, I'm hating the man who gave me Tyler. What is wrong with me?" she asked as she stepped back and out of his arms.

"Nothing." The space between them wasn't as wide as it once was, but he wished she had stayed in his arms. "Tell me what happened."

"As Tyler played with his new train, he mentioned that Santa hadn't brought him all his gifts. I asked what he meant, and he told me that his class had written letters to Santa, and he had asked for Santa to find his dad."

"I see, and you weren't aware of this letter."

"Nope. So I told him we'd talk after breakfast, then he took a bath, and while I was taking a shower, someone knocked on the door. I didn't know about it until I walked into the living room."

"Clint was in the living room?"

"Oh, no. No, no, no. Thank goodness. Tyler had opened the door when he didn't see anyone. The present was specifically for him, 'To Tyler, From Dad.' The rest is history. I called and blew up, hung up on him, would have slammed the phone if I'd had a landline."

David smiled. Pulling her back into his arms, "Rylee, you knew this might happen. We all did. God has a plan. You have to seek that plan. I know you think you have a better plan, but you don't—trust me."

Hanging on for dear life, Rylee hugged David and stepped away. "You're right. Right now it's really hard to see that, but I know it's true. Let's get to the house for lunch."

As they walked the path, they held hands, a team, a force that would face this as they moved forward. The kids had gotten used to them holding hands, so it was no big deal for the kids, but it provided the comfort they were needing at this point. Rylee trusted David not to send her in the wrong direction. He was a guy on whom she could count.

Walking into the house, David saw Tyler hugging Susie and comforting her. "What's wrong, Susie-girl?" he asked bending down to pick her up.

Susie sniffed up her tears and grabbed her daddy's neck, "Tyler found his daddy, but I still don't have a mommy." She then began to cry all the more.

David was dismayed. He thought the breakdowns were lessening for Susie. Would they ever go away? He motioned to Rylee, who was once again on the verge of tears, to stay with Marcie and Tyler while he talked to Susie. He led Susie down the hall to a back room and began, "Susie, how much did your Mommy love you?"

Sniffing once or twice, then rubbing the tears from her eyes she answered, "Mommy loved me to the moon and back."

"Would Mommy want you to be sad on this Christmas Day?"

"No."

"What are we celebrating today?" So far, this tactic was working.

"Jesus' birthday and Jesus and Mommy are in Heaven together."

"That is right! High-five!" They high-fived each other. "Now, no more tears. Let's be happy about what we have. You can always talk to Rylee if Daddy isn't enough."

"Can Rylee be my pretend Mommy?"

"Sweetheart, you need to ask her, not me." David knew Rylee would, but it would help Susie if she did the asking.

Both walked back into the kitchen where lunch was about to be served, buffet style. Everyone was lining up then taking their plates to the dining room, where two huge tables had been set up for lunch. The kids all sat at the kid's table, and all the adults sat at the main table. The main ranch house was decorated beautifully for Christmas. Golds and silvers were the colors used by the professional decorator David had recommend to the owner. The sideboard held turkey, duck, prime rib, and of course fried chicken for the kids. A mountain of mashed potatoes and cornbread dressing and gravy, along with macaroni and cheese, broccoli, and a huge garden salad. Everyone filled their plates more than once. Desserts brought by a few neighbors were on a bar in the kitchen pecan and pumpkin pie, banana pudding, and a cheesecake. Way too much food! But it was delicious.

By late afternoon, the kitchen was put back in order, and Tyler was asking if they could ride. David gathered all the children, and they rode around the arena for thirty minutes. The day had been perfect weather for a ride around the ranch, but time didn't permit.

Rylee and Tyler headed home after the sun went down. It had been a wonderful Christmas Day. David and Rylee had said their goodbyes before the kids were around and promised to talk the next day. Tyler, falling asleep on the way home, gave Rylee a continued chance to think. She had so much to pray about—Clint, David, her job. Oh Lord, I ask you to help me in the many decisions I need to make.

Thirteen

Tyler was getting so big, Rylee thought as she picked him up to carry him into the house when they returned from David's. Almost too big for her to carry anymore. Time had gotten away from her. Tyler was exhausted and never woke up, so she undressed him and put him in bed. It seemed her phone began ringing immediately. Trying to answer before it woke Tyler up, she whispered, "Hello."

"Why are you whispering?" David whispered back.

"Why are you whispering?" she asked, laughing at him. "I'm putting Tyler to bed, and he's sound asleep!" Rylee chuckled.

"Oh, I didn't realize I was whispering too!" He replied, laughing. "Just called to make sure you got home all right. I want to thank you for a wonderful afternoon and prepare you for Susie and her obsession with all things Mommy. She is going to ask you to be her mommy."

"Oh, she already has, and I said yes. I would love to be her Mommy. . . Ah, that sounds like a proposal which is not how I meant it at all." Rylee had a smile on her face and began humming . . . *Going to the Chapel* . . .

David thought it sounded pretty good, but kept his mouth shut. "I hope your Christmas brought you some peace. I know it began with some mountains and valleys, but I hope it ended on a good note. I'll see you sometime tomorrow. Thank you for being here."

"Thank you, David. We had a wonderful time. I wish you had told me I needed to bring a side dish. I wouldn't have minded."

"I didn't want you to feel you had to. No one cares if we bring one or not!"

Finishing their conversation, Rylee clicked off and sat down in the living room. Continuing to hum her song she began to wonder, once again, why had Clint done this? Did he not realize how it would send her guard up? When Tyler got up tomorrow, she knew he would have a hundred and one questions about his dad, and she would need to answer each one of them carefully.

∞ ∞ ∞

"But Mommy, why can't I call him and have him come over? If he's my daddy, this is his house too, right?"

"No, Tyler. That is not right. This is OUR house. You and I live here. We invite our friends over." Rylee had been talking with Tyler for over an hour.

"I want my daddy to come over!" Tyler stomped his foot and ran to his room, where he slammed his door.

Rylee slumped down, putting her head in her hands and couldn't believe this was the same sweet little boy who usually lived in this house. He had never acted this way before. Rylee thought, he doesn't even know Clint, and he's already acting like him.

Calling David, she wanted to put out an SOS for help. Maybe he could make Tyler understand. Tyler hadn't asked all the questions she thought he would. He wanted to know where he was and could he come over? Not why didn't you tell me about him, or anything? Just I want him, and I want him now.

"Hello, David."

"Hi, Rylee. It's a beautiful day in the neighborhood. How's your today going?"

"I'm sending out an SOS. Can you come over right now?" Rylee was all out of patience.

"Not this second. Can you give me an hour or so?" David could tell she was in dire need of help.

"I understand. I will see you when you get here. I know you're busy."

Rylee let Tyler stew in his room for a while. When she carefully opened the door, she didn't hear him. Apparently, he had climbed under his covers and fallen asleep. Closing the door carefully, she went to the couch and laid down.

She jokingly thought she could lock him in his room until he was grown, but that wouldn't work. Maybe locking Clint back in prison would help. This train of thought wasn't helping. Nothing productive came to her mind. So she prayed . . . and prayed. She was letting go, again, praying for an answer and praying for comfort in the situation. Praying for Clint to understand what he had unleashed—praying for patience to wait upon the Lord.

A light knock on the door jolted her upright. Looking out the window, she found David waiting for her to open up. "Hi, I'm sorry it took me so long."

"No, I'm sorry I demanded you come right that minute. I finally began praying about it, and I have calmed down. I think I can sit down with Tyler now and reason with him. He's just a little boy. He may think he knows it all, but he doesn't."

"Let's sit down and talk about this." Sitting on the front porch they began to talk about Tyler's needs and her needs.

"I need to be sure that when all this is finished, Tyler still knows I'm his mommy and I'm in charge."

David smiled, "You do know you won't always be in charge, in fact the only one in charge is Jesus."

Rylee turned to David, smiled, and took his hand. "Thank you for being reasonable. As you know, I just get a little wired up and go off the deep end."

David listened. "Do you think I can go in and talk with him man-to-man?"

"He was sleeping when I looked in earlier, but you're welcome to try." Rylee walked with him to Tyler's room.

David carefully opened the door and went inside. Rylee headed back to the living area.

"Rylee . . . Rylee, I thought you said he was in his room," David called her from the bedroom.

Rylee ran to Tyler's room, but Tyler was nowhere. He had never done anything like this. He must have gone out through the kitchen and went out that door. Running to the back door, she looked outside. There was Tyler, sitting on his swing, thinking.

Rylee ran outside and grabbed him off the swing, "I thought you'd run away!"

Tyler was fighting for breath under the heavy hugs, "Why would I do that? I need my mommy!"

David stood back and watched all unfold.

Rylee felt relief. Now maybe they could talk.

Tyler found his way out of his mom's arms and walked over to David. "Do you think we could talk? Mommy is too upset."

Rylee watched David and Tyler make their way back into the house. She sat on the swing and thought about all the changes that had taken place in just a short period of time. Bowing her head before the Almighty, she prayed for peace and wisdom in her current circumstances. Knowing that He would provide. After praying, she put a smile on her face and head into the house.

David and Tyler had gone to his room to talk, so Rylee began making cookies. In times of stress, EAT, she thought. Chocolate chip cookies seemed like the perfect solution. She softened the butter, added the brown and white sugar into the bowl and began to mix.

It took a little while at high speed to make sure the three ingredients were mixed well, then she added eggs, vanilla, baking soda, and flour. It wasn't long until it was time to add the best of the best chocolate chips. Putting two pans of cookie mounds into the oven set her tummy up for goodness coming soon. She couldn't wait to have a glass of milk and a warm cookie.

After the first batch was cooling, she heard what sounded like two men coming out of the cave for sustenance. Laughing to herself, she put two cookies on two plates and poured two glasses of milk. They pounced when they saw their snack. Sitting at the table, she asked, "Did you two have a good talk?"

Tyler looked at David before David spoke, "I think we did. Tyler wants to hear his birth story, and he knows you are the one who will share it with him. We talked about respect and honor toward our parents. That's what God designed, and if it's good enough for

God, it's even better for us. Tyler, you tell her what we talked about too."

Tyler looked at his mommy, "I'm sorry for the way I acted. It wasn't right to treat you like that, and David said it wasn't right for my bio . . . something father to send a present without your permission."

Rylee hugged her son and then hugged David. "Thank you, to both of you. I want you to know that after two chocolate chip cookies, I'm ready to discuss it all! How does that sound?"

"I guess that's my cue to go," David said.

"No, David, if you don't mind, I'd like you to stay." Rylee needed his support. Wherever this friendship was headed, she needed him around.

"Are you sure, Rylee? I'll understand if you'd like to be alone with Tyler." David didn't want to push his way into this situation.

"Please stay?" Tyler asked.

"All right, now let's have another cookie."

Fourteen

"Okay, buddy, where do you want to begin?" Rylee's stomach was jumping through hoops and shaking and grumbling.

"Where was I born?"

"I thought you knew where you were born. In a hospital in Davidson about thirteen miles from here."

"Where did you live?"

So far so good, Rylee thought to herself. "Well, I lived in a women's shelter in Davidson."

"Why didn't you live with my daddy?" Tyler seemed to have all his questions laid out in his head.

"We weren't together. I got pregnant with you before I graduated from high school. We tried living together, but it didn't work out." That was an understatement, she thought.

"Mommy, how come my daddy never came to see me? Does he not love me? Didn't he want me?" Tyler hung his head.

This was hard for a little boy to understand. Rylee thought it was unfair to make him go through this. "He cared, but he didn't live very close, he was so young, we both were. It took a long time for him to grow up."

"Does he want to see me now; does he want to know me?"

"Tyler I'm not sure, but I will ask and make sure you two meet. How does that sound?"

"Are you going to marry him? Can he live here?"

"I don't think so, Tyler. I'll set up for him to come over so you can meet him. Actually you've been introduced to him, you just didn't know it."

"Who was it?"

"Clint Owens, the guy you met at the mall." When his name came out of her mouth Rylee said a silent pray to God just hoping that Tyler asked no more questions.

"Oh, he had the blond, curly hair like mine." Tyler got up from the table and headed to his room. "Is it all right if I take my ball and glove and throw it around outside?"

"Of course. It's going to get colder so be sure and wear a light jacket."

"Okay, David, you want to throw the ball too?"

"Give me a minute, and I'll be right out." Tyler ran and got the ball and glove and went to the backyard. "Are you doing okay, Rylee? Do you need me to stay?"

"I'm surprisingly okay. He didn't ask a lot, but I'm sure he'll ask more." Lowering her head she said, "I'm sorry I dragged you into this. I just needed support."

Taking her hand and pulling her close he replied, "Rylee, I want to be involved. I feel . . . no, I have feelings for you. I don't know what they mean just yet or even if I'm ready to bring someone else into my world, but I do know that you are special. I will help with Tyler whenever you need me." With that he quickly gave her a sweet kiss on her forehead, and headed to the back yard.

As David headed out, Rylee thanked God for this man. He came into her life when she needed him most and she wasn't sure what she would do if he wasn't around.

Now what was she going to do? She had told Clint she would talk with Tyler. She had done that. now she would call him, first to tell him AGAIN how underhanded he was with the present, then, she would share what she told Tyler. Maybe she would invite him over for an hour one afternoon before school began in the new year.

∞ ∞ ∞

Clint knew he had overstepped with the present, but he couldn't help himself. He understood why Rylee was upset, but did she have to continue telling him what a jerk he had been? In the end he was going to see Tyler on Thursday after work. She had given him an hour, maybe he could stay longer if Tyler didn't want him to leave. He couldn't wait.

Thursday was quick in coming and promptly at five he was pulling in the driveway to see Tyler. He hadn't had time to clean up after work, but he figured kids don't care. Knocking on the door, he could see little eyes looking out the window.

Soon the door opened, and Tyler was standing there. Reaching out to hug him, Tyler pulled back. "Hey, kid, I'm your dad," Clint said as he walked into the house.

"I know." Tyler wasn't sure about this man.

Rylee asked Clint to sit down. Tyler continued.

"Why didn't you come to see me before today?" Tyler went right for the jugular.

Clint didn't expect such deep questions. "Well . . . part of the reason was I didn't know where you lived."

"What's my birthday?"

"I don't know. You're mother left, and I wasn't there." Clint wasn't taking all the blame.

"My mommy told me why she left. You could have found her and been there when I was born. Why weren't you?" Tyler needed some answers.

Rylee jumped into the conversation, "Tyler, these are good questions, but let's give Clint a little credit. He is here now."

"Thank you, Rylee. Just give me a chance, Tyler. I want to know you, find out when your birthday is and learn what you like and don't like."

"Okay, then why did you wait so long to find me?" Tyler didn't understand how a person could say they loved someone but not find them for their whole life.

"I don't know." Hanging his head, Clint realized how hard this would be to get to know this kid.

Tyler thought a minute, "Let's go play catch."

Clint was tired, he didn't want to play, "Not right now kid, maybe later. I've been working all day."

Tyler frowned. "Can you help me put my new train set together? It's in my bedroom. Mommy, can we go to my bedroom and work on my train?"

"Sure, Tyler. You all have fun. I'll be in the kitchen if you need me." Rylee got up and went to the kitchen. When she looked back in, they were still sitting on the couch. She wondered what that was all about. Waiting about five minutes she went back to the living room and they were still sitting. Tyler was slumped back in the chair and Clint was standing.

"I thought you two were going to go put a train together?"

"No, I have to be going. I'll come back another time, if you will let me."

"I'll let you know." Walking Clint to the door, Tyler stayed in his chair. "Thank you for coming." Rylee began to close the door.

"Goodbye, Tyler."

Tyler said nothing.

"Does he have to come back?" Tyler asked Rylee. "He said he was my daddy, but he didn't act like David does when he is around. David always talks to me, not you know, like I'm not there. Oh, Mom, I don't know, he just didn't act like I thought a dad would act — like David."

Rylee wasn't sure what went on the ten minutes they were alone, but it must not have been good. "I think we can't judge one visit. We need at least two or three. What happened?"

"He wasn't nice. I want a daddy who is nice. After you left he said he didn't like trains and really needed to go. I just sat here. He never said it was nice to meet me or when is your birthday? Maybe he doesn't care?"

Rylee's heart broke. She needed to be very careful with what she said. "You know, Tyler, he was probably just as nervous as you were. You kind of came at him with both fists. Just like he needs to get to know you, you need to get to know him. Maybe next time you could ask questions about him."

Tyler nodded his head, "That sounds good. Maybe next time."

Rylee smiled. She'd like to wring Clint's neck! She couldn't wait to give him a call.

"Hey kiddo, let's go play catch."

"You're the greatest Mommy, thanks."

Fifteen

Three days before they were to go back to school, Rylee called Clint. She had waited for him to call but no response. She hoped he was thinking over the last visit and planning the next one, but she couldn't be sure.

Calling his number, he picked up after the first ring. "Clint, I was surprised I didn't hear from you after your visit," she was brutally honest.

"Wasn't sure you wanted me to call? Visit didn't go as I had planned."

"Maybe that was the problem; you planned the visit. You can't plan a visit with a five-year-old. Why don't you stop by on Saturday morning for an hour, unplanned, unannounced? I'll be the only one to know you're on your way. How about ten?"

"Let me think about it?" Clint didn't want a repeat of the last visit.

"What's there to think about? Do you want to know Tyler or not? If not, then lose this phone number and our address." Rylee was angry. "Don't walk into my child's life and then not worry about walking out."

"Okay, I'll be there." Clint honestly didn't know what to do. He had no clue what a real family was or could be.

∞∞∞

Hanging up the phone, he thought back to his life with his parents when he was Tyler's age. He and his little brother grew up in an ordinary house, he guessed. Typical for them anyway. His dad worked at a factory, and his mom stayed home with the boys. They partied, but what parents didn't, he thought.

School was relatively easy, but when he got to middle school, he found football, and that was his number one subject. It was also the one thing his father never let up about. If he did anything wrong, he was yelled at, cussed at sometimes, and overall made to feel like he didn't deserve to play. He had tried telling his dad that it made him feel bad, but his dad would slap the top of his head and tell him to grow a pair.

As middle school grew to a close, Clint had become more and more aggressive on the football field. When he went to high school, he was immediately put on the varsity team. He wasn't tall, but he was strong and could run, so it didn't take much for him to start his aggression on the other team.

During one game, the referee kicked him out for unnecessary roughness, but his dad praised him for his toughness. He was the #1 stud in high school, and all the girls wanted a piece of the pie. He had a different girl every night, then Rylee got pregnant his senior year. They tried living together, but his only outlet for his aggression was Rylee, and he took it all out on her.

One morning when he woke up, she was gone. He had never found her, but he didn't care, one less thing to worry about. He was always hoping for a chance at college ball, but no one offered, so he got a job bussing tables at a local restaurant, and from there, he ended up in prison.

What a life, a miserable life — that was until he started counseling, and he'd gotten better. Raise a kid, he thought. Heck, he didn't even know how to get along with one. His dad hadn't taught him anything except degrade and hit.

If he wanted to see Tyler, maybe he needed some parenting classes. So he called the county human welfare services and asked. Classes were Tuesday night at 6 p.m. When they asked him how old the child was and they seemed surprised as he replied Tyler was five years old. However, he felt he made a good decision.

∞∞∞

Saturday morning came, and there was a light knock at the door. Tyler was sitting on the couch watching cartoons and looked out the window.

"Mommy, it's that man, my dad. He's at the door." Tyler was surprised to see him.

"Well, answer the door, Tyler, and be nice." Rylee looked at the clock. It was precisely ten. Peeking out of the kitchen, she watched as Tyler opened the door and let Clint come in.

"Good morning, Tyler," Clint said as he came through the door.

"Hi, what are you doing here?" Tyler wasn't excited on the outside, but inside he was glad to see him again.

"Well, I think the other day didn't go very well, so I wanted to try again, but first, I need to apologize for being a jerk. This being a father is new to me. I guess I forgot that it would be new to you too."

"Oh." Tyler thought about David. "I have David, and he says I'm his little boy. But I don't call him daddy."

Clint didn't react to the comment about David, even though his heart dropped a little. "Tyler, could you teach me to be a better dad? What should a dad do? What should I know?"

"My birthday!" Tyler could fill him in quickly. "It's April seventh. I'll be six! My favorite thing is trains, Santa brought me a train for Christmas, and I need help putting it together. I love hot dogs. Do you like hot dogs?"

Clint began, "April seventh, got it! Trains, yes, I will help. Hot dogs — only if you add chili!"

Tyler began to laugh, and Rylee sighed in relief. "Let's play ball. I'll go get my glove and ball you got me."

"Sounds good, Tyler."

Rylee walked into the room. "Thank you for showing up and making an effort. About eleven, you need to find a reason to leave, then we'll make another time for you to see him."

Clint nodded okay. "I wanted to tell you I signed up for parenting classes at the human services department. I hope they give me some clues on how to talk to Tyler."

"I thought you did just fine." She glanced over at Tyler as he walked back into the room. "Well, look who we have here. Mr. Baseball himself. You all have fun but stay in the yard."

"Yes, Mommy." Tyler went running through the open door. "Come on, Clint."

It didn't take long until Clint was showing Tyler the correct way to hold the bat. She watched from the living room, keeping her eye on the clock. At five past eleven, Clint waved goodbye. Tyler ran into the living area and said, "I had a lot of fun, Mommy. I guess Clint can be fun too. Now can I go to my horseback riding lessons?"

"Sounds good. Let me call David to make sure he's ready for you, all right?" Rylee wanted to talk to him about Clint coming over again.

"Do I need to change?" Tyler was wearing workout pants and a sweatshirt.

"Maybe put on a pair of jeans!"

Tyler ran to his room, and Rylee called David. "Hey dude, are you ready for Tyler's riding lessons?" Rylee was ready to see David. She needed one of his generous hugs and sweet kisses. He always made her feel like she was number one in his heart.

"Yes, ma'am, come on out. I'm anxious to see you. Oh, and Tyler!" David was glad to hear from them.

"Clint came back today. It went pretty well. We'll talk about it after his lesson." They hung up, and Rylee grabbed her jacket as Tyler headed for the door.

"Come on, Mommy. We don't want to be late."

Sixteen

Rylee was looking forward to seeing David. They both had been super busy, and phone calls were close to nonexistent this week. She hadn't realized just how close they had become. Making sure she had fixed her hair and added a little lipstick to her lips, they were on their way to the ranch.

"Hey, David," Rylee had just pulled up, and she and Tyler got out of the car.

"It's been a while," David put his arm around her waist and pulled her towards him. Kissing the top of her head, they walked toward the barn. "I've missed you, Rylee."

Hugging him tightly, she said, "I've missed you too. I don't think we've gone an entire week before without seeing each other, and I don't like it when we do!" Rylee continued, "How long are you going to work with him? I thought I might go over to your house and see the girls. I've missed their sweet chatter. I brought them each a little something."

"They'd like that. Marcie is keeping an eye on Susie, so have fun." David loved that Rylee was always thinking of the girls.

Giving each other a hug, Rylee walked the short distance to David's comfortable log home. It was large, and it was very comfortable. Rylee knew David was happy he didn't have to share a bathroom with his girls.

"Knock, Knock," Rylee opened the door and walked inside. "Marcie, it's Rylee." No answer. Rylee called out again, but no one answered. Walking to the back of the house Rylee could hear Susie talking.

"Marcie, Daddy's gonna be mad when he sees all that on you. You better wash up before he gets home."

"Be quiet, I'm just practicing for when we go to school. All the girls are wearing makeup, and I want to also. Just you keep quiet."

Rylee smiled. Oh those teen years, she thought. Rounding the corner she saw Marcie and cleared her throat, "Need help?"

Susie jumped right in, "Daddy's going to be so mad."

Marcie knew Susie was right and stopped. "Oh Rylee, could you help me? Daddy's going to kill me for sure."

By the time Marcie and Rylee were finished, Marcie had a small amount of clear lip gloss and a little powder to take away the shine.

"Oh, Rylee, I love it. Thank you so much." Marcie grabbed Rylee and hugged her hard.

"No problem. Let's go see if Tyler is finished. I bet David will like what you've done."

Grabbing Susie's hand, they walked back to the barn and arrived about the time that Tyler finished. Before David could say a word . . . Rylee jumped in . . . "Don't you like what Marcie has done to her look? Now that she is old enough to wear a little lip gloss and some powder, it brightens up that beautiful face."

David took Rylee's cue, "Looks great, Marcie. Oh and Susie, did you put a little lip gloss on too?"

"Yes, Daddy," Susie and Marcie smiled, "We're glad you like it."

Rylee walked over and gave David a kiss on his cheek, looking up into his golden-brown eyes she said, "I wish we could stay longer, but the day is late, and we go back to school next week, so there is lots to do."

David held on tight, "Would you like to go to dinner tomorrow night?"

"I'd love to. What time? I'll have to find someone to watch Tyler." Rylee was still looking deep in his eyes.

"Bring him here, and I'll hire a nanny to watch them. Around six, here tomorrow night."

"I can't wait."

It took Rylee a little bit on the way home to come back to earth. She wanted to see what Tyler was thinking.

"Tyler."

"Yes."

"Did you enjoy your visitor today?"

"Yeah, it was okay. If David had been there, it would have been great. I love David. He always makes me feel special."

Rylee couldn't believe her ears. Tyler sounded like he would have preferred David's company. "But I thought you were anxious to meet your birth dad? That's the whole reason why I'm allowing Clint to come over."

"Mom," he called her instead of Mommy since he would be six soon, "I want to know my birth dad, but he's ONLY my birth dad, not my real daddy."

"Well, all right, but I think you need to get to know Clint a little better, and he is making an effort. You know Jesus tells us that when we receive Him, we are changed. Maybe Clint has accepted Jesus, and that's why he has changed and wants to know you more."

"Mom, I love you, I've got all I ever wanted, and that was to meet my real dad."

"He's going to take us to eat hamburgers at the Frosty Cream next Thursday. He called and asked if we would go, I figured that would make you happy, so we're going."

Tyler got out of the car and slammed the door, "Okay!" Running into the house, he grabbed his ball and glove but was met with resistance from his mom.

"Nope, you have to clean that room, take a shower, read your Sunday School assignment and get to bed. Tomorrow is church."

Tyler turned and went back into the house as Rylee picked up some items she had left in the car's trunk. She was tired. Clint's visit had taken a lot out of her, but going to the ranch for Tyler's horseback riding lessons had its perks. Mainly being with David, and she was getting so comfortable with him.

Going to church always refreshed her. She felt so close to God when she entered the sanctuary. On Sunday mornings, she would get up early and read her daily devotional. One thing she enjoyed was listening to music, prayer, then she would read. She wanted to make sure she was focused solely on Jesus before she spent time in the Word. He was the most important person in her life. Without

Jesus, she would never have survived Tyler's birth or the years in school. He never let her down or broke any of His promises. It was so joyful to know He was always there.

Her prayer this morning focused on Tyler and Clint. She had been worried about bringing Clint back into their lives, but the Holy Spirit had given her peace about it, and it seemed to be going well. She prayed that Tyler would understand that Clint wanted to know him better and that Tyler would give him a chance. She added a few prayers for David, Susie, and Marcie. They were good people. She loved having them in her life. David had stirred something inside of her that she hadn't felt in a very long time.

The church was packed when she and Tyler entered the back of the sanctuary. Seeing Clint, she went over and welcomed him to church.

Tyler jumped into the conversation, "Hey, are we going to eat hamburgers this Thursday as Mom said?"

"If you want to, I've invited you to, but I don't want to force you." Clint was hoping Tyler would be excited.

"Oh, I want to go. I love their chocolate shakes. Can I have one of those too!?"

Clint laughed.

Rylee smiled and moved Tyler down the aisle to where they usually sat.

David watched the interaction and hoped Rylee was not feeling cornered.

"Hey, I thought maybe you two were going to sit with Clint," David spoke up as they entered the pew.

Rylee smiled, "Nope, gotta sit where I always sit; otherwise, I'll be in someone's place." She began laughing. "You know how Baptists are!"

"You're such a joker," David said to her as the congregation stood for prayer and singing.

∞∞∞

After church, David invited Tyler to go home for some horse-back riding. Then Tyler could stay with the girls while David and Rylee went to dinner. She needed to rest . . . she may only be twenty-three, but she seemed to be burning the candle at both ends and she needed a — Calgon take me away moment! It amazed her sometimes that she could remember really old commercials.

Waving to them as they left, Rylee breathed a sigh of relief. The first thing she was going to do was take a long, hot shower just for the heck of it and a nap. Then she could get things ready for the week. Arriving home, she didn't disappoint herself. Immediately after she walked into the house, she was in the shower allowing the hot water to wash over her and easing the tension of her muscles, slowly relaxing her mind. Thirty minutes later, she was wrapped up in her robe and laying on the bed sound asleep.

She didn't know how long she had been asleep when she heard someone at the front door. Looking out the bedroom window, she saw the car that Clint had been driving. Now, what does he want? she thought. Being nice can only go so far when you're worn out. Right? Walking to the door, she asked him, "What do you want, Clint?"

"Can you open the door?"

"No, I can't. I just got out of the shower. What do you need? Tyler isn't here."

"I want to talk. Can you get dressed, and then we can talk?"

Rylee hung her head in defeat. "Sit down on the porch, and I'll be right out." Walking back to her room, she quickly put on jeans and a T-shirt thinking, This better be good.

Opening the door, she walked out on the porch before he could come inside. "What do we need to talk about?"

Clint wasn't really communicative. He stayed quiet until she pushed it.

"Clint, why are you here?" Rylee wasn't putting up with this.

"My job is over at the end of the week, and I won't be around for about six to eight weeks. Are you still going to let me see Tyler when I get back?"

"If he wants to see you, he can see you. You can always call him." Rylee wasn't going to force her son to do anything.

"He's not the only one I was hoping would be glad to see me come back. Maybe we could see how this would go, you and me back together. I know I messed up, but you're a fine woman, and I'd love for us to get together."

Rylee almost burst out laughing. She sat quietly for a few minutes, just staring out into the yard. The trees were so bare at this time of year, but they would bud out in another month or two, and spring would be upon them. Finally, taking a deep breath, she began. "There are so many things wrong with that statement or request. First, there is no us. You asked to be in Tyler's life, and I'm allowing it for now. It doesn't matter what you think, I am in control of my life, and I won't let that change. I know you meant it as a compliment, but have you forgotten what you put me through before Tyler was born."

"No, I haven't forgotten. I guess I thought you might see me in a different light. I found Jesus. I go to church. I'm trying hard to learn what it means to be a good man. I thank you for letting me see Tyler, but when I think back to what we had . . ."

"Clint, we were in high school. What we thought was love was only lust." Rylee chuckled. "You were not just lusting after me but every girl in school."

Clint laughed too. "You're right. I didn't want to pass up a good thing. But I know times are different. I want us to communicate and to be friends."

"I think we can do that but nothing else."

Clint stood to leave, "Can I at least hug you? You've given me such a sweet little boy. You have done a good job, Rylee. I wish I could have done better." Taking Rylee's hand, he pulled her close and enveloped her in his arms for a quick hug.

She hugged him, too, and said goodbye. "You have our phone number. If you want to talk to Tyler, just call. We'll still see you Thursday, right?"

"Yes, I want to explain to Tyler."

Clint waved as he drove away.

Rylee sat back down on the porch and smiled. Maybe he would

grow up a little each time she saw him.

∞∞∞

David came a little early to pick up Rylee for their dinner date. The nanny had arrived early, so he just left. As he arrived, he saw Clint and Rylee on the porch, hugging. Was there more to this than he knew? Surely not? He wasn't going to pursue a relationship that would fail. He couldn't handle it. He knew what Rylee had told him about Clint, and he didn't understand the hug.

Calling Rylee from his car, he asked, "Are you ready? I'm about at your house? Now why was he lying to her.

"Yes, I am and eager also!" Rylee had high hopes for this date.

David knocked on the door as Rylee opened it.

"How did Tyler's lesson go this afternoon?" Rylee asked as they were leaving.

David didn't say much which was so not like him. "Fine."

"Is there something wrong?"

"I just have a pounding headache. I'm sorry, I shouldn't take it out on you." David hated that he kept adding to the lies.

"Maybe we just need to cancel, David. I don't want it to get any worse for you." Rylee was worried about him.

"Would you mind? Tyler can just spend the night, and I'll bring him home in the morning early so he can get ready for school." Lies, Lies, Lies.

"That's fine. Would you like to come in for a minute? I was so looking forward to tonight. I hope you start feeling better." Rylee was upset.

"I think I'll just go home. Thank you, Rylee."

"No problem."

Seventeen

Tuesday at school was so hectic, head lice had made their entrance into the building, and Rylee was left to call parents to pick their children up from school. Rylee was glad when Tyler came running into her office after David dropped him off.

"Mom, is tonight choir?" Tyler loved going to choir. He had a sweet natural voice that she just loved.

"Yes, it is. Are Susie and Marcie going? I haven't talked with Marcie all day." Rylee thought that was strange, but she didn't make too much of it.

"Susie said she had to go to . . . somewhere, but I forgot."

"That's okay. I'm sure David will let me know that I need to pick you up. If you're ready, then let's go home." Tyler chased her to the parking lot, and they giggled all the way there. Rylee laughed and grabbed her son, and swung him around. "I love you so much, Tyler."

"I love you too, Mom."

∞∞∞

David knew he should call Rylee. He wasn't bringing Tyler home from choir, and that was his responsibility. Picking up the phone, he decided he'd text her.

David – *You'll need to pick Tyler up from choir. The girls and I will be out of town.*

Rylee – *Is something wrong?*

David – *No, just a busy time. I'll talk to you later.*

David felt like he was dishonest, and he was. He should pick up the phone and tell Rylee how he felt when he saw her hugging

Clint. He was acting like a child. He was worse than a child. His girls didn't understand why they weren't going to choir. He even lied to them about picking something up in a nearby town. He hated himself right now.

He didn't want to miss Bible Study on Wednesday, so he bribed them with that. He would definitely tell Rylee about what he saw and how it bothered him. Definitely!

It was strange picking up Tyler at choir. David had been picking him up since September, and here it was the first part of January, and she was doing it for the first time. She had scolded herself for thinking anything was wrong. David had work to do, but it hadn't stopped him before. He could pull his children out of the program when he needed to. They were working on the Children's Easter program, and Marcie had a big singing part. Missing one practice wouldn't kill her. She did wonder if he would skip Bible Study.

The next morning as Rylee walked into work, her phone rang. "Hello."

"Good morning. This is Clint. I wanted to let you know that I have a little time this evening to see Tyler. I'm leaving for Montana on Saturday and will be gone for at least three months. I want to tell him personally."

"Can't we wait until tomorrow night. Remember we're meeting at the Frosty Cream for hamburgers and shakes?"

"I know, but the more I see him the better."

"You could come to the church at five thirty for supper."

"That works great. I'll see you both then." Clint was glad that would work out.

The day was typical for the spring semester: checking on new sixth graders coming in the fall and making sure all shot records were current. She would send out notices to all parents of incoming students, so they had plenty of time to get up-to-date.

That night she and Tyler arrived at church, and immediately Tyler saw Clint. "What's he doing here?" Leave it to Tyler to say what's on his mind.

"Well," Rylee began, "his job is moving him, and he wants to talk to you. I invited him to come and have supper."

"Oh, I guess that's all right." Tyler wanted to sit with David and the girls like they always did. "Do we have to sit with him?"

"He can sit with us!" Rylee responded to her rude little boy. "He will sit with everyone. Is that all right? Now be nice, Tyler." Rylee was not happy with her son.

Seeing the girls walking into the gym, Tyler ran to them. Rylee saw David about the same time David saw Clint.

"Hey, David. We're sitting over here. Come join us." Rylee thought David was hesitating, but then he walked on over.

"Hi, Clint. What made you decide to join us tonight?" David really was uncomfortable.

Rylee said, "Oh, I didn't get to tell you that Clint is leaving for a few months and wanted to tell Tyler goodbye."

"I've got another job in Montana. I'll be gone at least three months, Tyler. I wanted to tell you personally and have a meal with you before I left."

Tyler just looked at Clint. "Ah, okay. Why?"

"Well, the man I work for travels around America and builds large office buildings. His next job is in Montana."

"That's cool. You get to see a lot of different places. Will you come to see me when you come back?"

"Of course. I'll call you, too, or you can call me; just ask your mother first." Clint knew this was all up to Rylee. He wouldn't be calling if Rylee didn't allow it.

Dinner that night was spaghetti and salad, tea, bread, and of course chocolate cake—a typical Wednesday night at the Baptist church. Pastor Park came by and met Clint, inviting him back when Clint returned.

As Clint prepared to leave, he took Tyler aside. "Kid, I've enjoyed getting to know you. We'll have more things to do when I get back. Can I have a hug?"

Tyler hugged him and stood back. "Be careful, Dad."

Clint's eyes filled up, but he didn't let them spill over. "I will, son."

∞∞∞

As Rylee and David walked over to the Bible Study, David felt confession would be good for his soul. "When I came to pick you up on Sunday, I saw Clint there. I didn't want to interrupt, so I just kept going and went around the block." He laughed at her look. "I saw Clint grab you and hug you. You had your arms around him too. I thought maybe you two had gotten together. I didn't know what to do."

"Oh, David. You're silly. I can barely stand him, but I can forgive him just like Jesus forgave me. All of us can be redeemed, and I believe Clint is on the way. I'm so relieved that he is leaving for a while. He wears me out. Really. For someone who never cared, he started doing a lot of caring, quick. Is that why you had a headache and went home?"

David laughed. "Yes, but I was dying to tell you what a jerk I was." Taking Rylee's hand, they continued the trip to the fellowship hall. Bible Study that night was extra sweet. It was all about the saving power of Jesus. David was glad he had come.

Eighteen

Easter fell early in April, the children's choir was performing, Marcie was nervous about her solo. The children dressed in their Easter dresses and slacks looked so nice standing in front of the congregation, poised and ready. The music was beautiful, David was one proud dad, and Rylee couldn't believe how sweet the younger choir sang. It brought tears to her eyes to see her young boy growing up.

The preacher's sermon reminded everyone of the sacrifice that Jesus made for each of us, and when the call to the altar took place, David, Marcie, and Susie joined the church. The congregation was excited. They had come to know the Hunt family and loved them dearly. After the service, everyone, Rylee, David, and the kids went to a local BBQ restaurant for lunch and to celebrate Tyler's sixth birthday. They had a grand time, and Tyler was the star of the day.

The weather was beautiful in Waterstown that May. The Bradford Pear trees were in bloom throughout the town, and the flowers were adding a plethora of colors to the downtown median. Waterstown was enjoying the weather. The Community Choir would be performing at the Old Restored Church for the next three Sunday afternoons. The high school One Act Play was performing on Saturday nights on stage at Trollinger Park. Many of the area clubs and churches were sponsoring events throughout the summer months. Graduation was almost here for the high school seniors, and Rylee was ready to be at home and relaxing for the summer.

As the end of school drew near, Tyler brought home a flyer about joining the local baseball teams. He was so excited. Rylee told him they'd talk about it, but when David took them out for ice cream after the play that night, Tyler was excited when David said he'd help with Tyler's team if he was allowed to play.

The last day of school was hectic. Tyler was excited when he and Susie ran into her office after school.

"We're both gonna be in first grade, Mom!"

"We passed, we passed!" Yelled Susie.

"Was there any doubt? You two were the smartest in the group. I'm surprised you aren't in high school," she said, laughing and smiling at their enthusiasm.

David walked in and agreed, they both should be in advanced first-grade classrooms next year.

Everyone was excited. Marcie would be in eighth grade, and she had grown up so much during the year. She was almost as tall as her dad and embarrassed that she was taller than most of the boys.

"Why don't we plan a picnic after church on Sunday? Everyone can meet at the farm – we'll ride the horses and go to our favorite place." Marcie was excited about her idea. "Maybe we could go to the swimming pond and swim after we eat. Please, Daddy, please."

Everyone began begging to go on a picnic.

Rylee chimed in. "This is up to David. If he has time, then Tyler and I will join you all."

"Then we're doing it!" yelled David as he attempted to jump around like the kids.

"Slow down, Daddy. You're too old to jump around too much!" Marcie said and then followed the other kids who were running to the car.

"David, if this is too much, please tell me." Rylee didn't want to overwhelm him. "I mean, it's been so long since I rode a horse."

"I think it's a great idea. I'm just wondering what you will ride. Would you mind riding double with me?"

"I don't have a problem with it. Why?"

"Well, Clara always wanted her own horse. She never felt safe riding with me. I didn't know how you would feel."

"I think it sounds . . . cozy!" Then she blushed. "You know what I mean."

Arriving at their cars, Rylee said, "Let me know what time, and we'll be there. I can bring the lunch."

"No, the cook at the ranch will put a big basket together. That's what she loves to do. I'll see you at church Sunday, and then we'll decide on a time, bye."

Rylee was excited. Talking with David and hearing bits and pieces about his wife, Clara, made her want to know more. She'd made up her mind that if they were going to try out this relationship, then they both needed to share more with each other. Heavens, she'd even forgotten his wife's name until he mentioned her. Yes, she would make a point of asking for more stories about Clara. The girls needed that.

∞∞∞

As David drove out of the parking lot and headed home, he thought more and more about Rylee. He knew she was younger than him by several years. David had gone to vet school, and she had gone to nursing school, but she couldn't be much older than twenty-three. She seemed older, an old soul in a young body. A lovely, young body, he thought.

"Oh, Lord," he said to himself, "this young lady is all I think about all the time. Please give me the right thoughts. Help me to get to know her better."

He didn't want to get personal, but they had gotten closer during the school year. He had let Rylee know he was interested up to a point. Maybe it was time. He would get to know her better at the picnic. Heavens they'd seen each other consistently over the last nine months, and he still didn't know much about her. Funny how age didn't matter once you weren't a teenager anymore. Now it's time to get to learn more.

On the way to church that Sunday, David had decided to talk to

Pastor Park about his feelings for Rylee. Maybe a little counseling would help him. They got to church and once the girls saw Rylee, they went running toward her. Here we go, he thought.

∞∞∞

David had been on Rylee's mind since Friday. Maybe she was entering an area that she didn't want to go to. She had been attracted to him since they first met. She hoped he knew that, but still, they were just friends. He was always polite. She had never known anyone like him. She knew he was special.

She remembered the first time she saw him at school with Marcie. She remembered how soft his hands looked and how clean they were. Her dad had been a mechanic, and his hands always had a greasy look. He was a little taller than herself, about five foot ten. His eyes, oh his eyes, were golden brown like the sky at sunset. Warm and wonderful. She had guessed him to be around thirty. She still didn't know how old he was; maybe she should ask. She thought she might sit down with the pastor and talk about this unusual relationship. She would ask him today. Perhaps they could meet next week.

The service that day was putting God first in our lives. Brother Curt talked about the Israelites in the wilderness and God's command to put no other God before Him. They didn't listen, and things didn't turn out as God wanted. He reminded the congregation that many of us do the same thing. We forget that God is or should be our number one. When that happens, God's plan for our life is thwarted, and what good things He planned for us don't happen at that time. When we refuse to honor God and follow His wisdom in our decisions, it causes us to become bogged down. In our culture, this behavior causes a decline in our moral standards and attitudes.

Wise words, Rylee thought. She knew she would talk to him this week. It was essential for all parts of her life.

David listened as Pastor Park talked about putting God first in our lives. He knew what he said was so true, but David felt like he hadn't kept up his end of that in the last several years since Clara had passed. David had let life get in his way of honoring God. Yes, he needed to talk with the preacher. Hopefully, a little counseling would set him on the right path, he thought.

After the services, they spoke briefly about the picnic, and then Rylee and Tyler got in their car and headed home. Tyler wanted to take his ball and glove in case they might play ball. He also wanted to take his bug jar that he used to hunt down unusual bugs. Bugs became a new obsession for Tyler. Not one Rylee enjoyed, but boys would be boys. At least it wasn't snakes, not yet anyway.

Heading to the ranch Rylee was excited. She had spoken with the pastor after church, and they would meet on Tuesday afternoon. She prayed that the meeting would help to clear her mind. Right now, she was ready for a picnic.

Nineteen

Sunday afternoon was beautiful. Texas weather in May can be a little warm, but today the sky was blue, and the temperature was a pleasant seventy-eight degrees. No wind and not many insects yet. As they saddled up, David asked Rylee, "You want to ride in front or back? Either way, you'll have to hold on!"

"Whichever is most comfortable for you, David. Why don't I try riding behind? It may be a little bumpy, but I think I can handle it."

David smiled, "Let's get the kids saddled up and put Marcie in charge of Tyler, then we'll be ready to go."

Rylee hung around and watched the kids. It seemed like it was natural for them. Maybe one day, it would feel the same for her. She had packed a few towels, and they wore their bathing suits under their clothes.

"Everybody ready?" David asked, helping Rylee swing up behind him she grabbed his waist and held on tight.

"Let's go, Daddy. I'm getting hungry," said Susie, and she spurred her horse forward.

Marcie knew where they were going, so she and Tyler led the way. Holding onto David tightly gave Rylee a good bit of knowledge about how muscular David was. She didn't realize how riding horses might toughen up the midsection. Nice six-pack, she thought.

Riding across the fields was a lot of work; at least staying on the horse was for her. This gave her a reason to hold on even tighter. The kids were having a good time, and Tyler looked like an old pro riding across the field. Rylee had needed this. She felt free and was loving it. Across a field, she saw a large group of trees around a large pond. Rylee thought this must be where they were headed. Beautiful, she thought. Great place for a romantic getaway!

Once they all arrived, the unpacking began. The girls tied horses up to a tree and unloaded their saddlebags. Juices, water, tablecloth, and several containers full of delightful food, Rylee surmised as she smelled their flavors wafting her way. David had her hold Black Beard while he unloaded the rest of the food and took him over to tie to a tree in the shade.

"Hey guys, do you want to play ball?" Tyler called to everyone.

"Why don't you and Susie throw the ball to me while Rylee and Marcie get the food out? We can all sit around and eat, relax and maybe do a little swimming in the pond."

Rylee was a little worried about Tyler getting in the pond. "Aren't there snakes in the pond?"

"And fish and worms and bugs. He'll be okay if he leaves them alone. The pond is pretty low so that they can walk across it."

Rylee and Marcie laid the tablecloth on top of the three blankets they had put down. This way, no one had to sit on the itchy grass area. Marcie was in charge, telling Rylee where she should put the food. She had done this so much, and the little mother in her came out quite well.

"Come and get it!" she called to her dad, Susie, and Tyler.

Rylee spoke up, "Thank you, Marcie. You did an excellent job of putting everything out. I'll do the cleanup while you and the others go swimming after lunch."

"Wow, this looks so good. Thanks, Rylee." David said, and Marcie's face fell.

"Oh, I didn't do this, David. Your daughter was completely in charge. Thank her. She's the one who deserves the honor!"

Marcie blushed as her daddy picked her up and swung her around. "I love you, little one. Thanks."

The chicken sandwiches, coleslaw, and cupcakes, along with the lemonade, the sun, and then the swim, made everyone a little lazy. Tyler, Susie, and Marcie went looking for objects for their craft projects. Rylee and David sat with their backs against a tree and talked. They hadn't had time to talk.

"May I ask you a few questions personal questions, David? You don't have to answer if you prefer not to, but although I've known you for the past nine months or so, we still know so little about each other."

"I've thought the same thing. I don't even know how old you are, Rylee."

Rylee laughed, "How old do you think?"

"That's a loaded question to answer. You share!" he replied, laughing and feigning terror.

"I turned twenty-three last month, and no, I'm not a baby! Now, how old are you? Not that it matters, I like you just the way you are. Ugh, that sounded like a song." Rylee shrugged her shoulders and smiled.

"I'm ancient in comparison to you. I'm thirty-three. It took me a while to come to terms with my age, which is silly, but here I am." David quietly sat there waiting for the next question. The sun was shining down on Rylee, and he thought she almost looked angelic! He remembered the first time he met her. All business-like as a first-time school nurse.

"I'm not sure how to ask this question, but I'd like to know more about Clara. I know you loved her and that you and the girls still grieve, but I know nothing about her." Rylee hoped that didn't upset David that she had asked.

"Gosh, where do I begin?

"I'd like to see a picture," Rylee said.

"Oh, let me look." David dug in his wallet and found the picture he loved the most. "She had just given birth to Susie. Both the girls are in this picture." He handed the photo to Rylee as he continued. "She was sixteen when we met. We dated until she was eighteen, then we got married. She worked while I attended college and then vet school. Clara was quiet. She thought deeply, a lot like you do at times. She loved staying home with the girls and loved being room mom to Marcie's class. Great cook, but she couldn't keep the house worth a darn!" Laughing. "I took over that job quickly."

Rylee smiled, "She sounds wonderful for you. When did she find out she was sick?"

"About three years after Susie was born. Clara went for her check-up, and her blood work was suspect. That began the rounds of doctors and tests. They soon discovered she had stage four colon cancer, and they gave her six months."

Rylee reached out for David's hand, her eyes filling with tears. "I'm so sorry, David."

"I know. She gave it her best, but within three months, she was gone. Susie was two and a half and doesn't even remember her except through pictures. Marcie was just ten, and it hit her hard. We went to grief counseling which helped."

"Daddy, look what we found." Susie and Tyler came running with Marcie in tow.

That ended their talk, but Rylee understood the family unit a little more. She was glad they had taken the time to know each other a bit better. Maybe there was hope for them. She'd wait and see.

"What is it?" David called.

"Come on. We have to show you."

Grabbing Rylee's hand, he pulled her up, and they went running after the kids, holding her hand the entire time. Finally, they came upon an old skull, a cow skull, that excited the kids.

"Can we take it home and paint it and put jewels all over it? Then we can hang it in the barn. Please." Marcie and Susie were very convincing.

"Of course. Let's grab the tablecloth and we'll wrap it up then Rylee, if she doesn't mind, can carry it on the way home. Now it's time to load up and ride home. Let's go. It's getting late."

It took them about twenty minutes to clean and pack everything they brought, including their trash and treasures. The kids' horses were loaded down, and once in the saddle, they took off. David pulled Rylee up on his horse, only he put her in front this time.

"Now you can see where we are going. Thought you might like that, plus if you're in the saddle, you might enjoy the ride better."

As they rode, her long hair took its toll on his face. Finally, he tucked the flying strands inside her shirt, and as he did, he gently kissed the back of her neck. Chills ran down her arms, and she quickly wished he'd do it again.

David wanted to kiss her again, but the kids were near, and he didn't want to take advantage. He knew they had more time. He couldn't wait to talk with the pastor to see what his thoughts would be.

Twenty

David was nervous as he entered the church office for his meeting with the pastor. He knew that was silly, but he didn't want the pastor to tell him he should wait longer or forget her although he knew the pastor would let that be David decision. He had prayed for the preacher to guide him in the direction he should move, and he was determined to follow that, no matter what he wanted.

Walking into the Pastor Park's office, David and the pastor shook hands. The pastor knew that David was nervous, so he led with prayer. Reassuring David this was God's doing, and no one else could interfere.

"David, I know what you said when you set up this meeting. Why don't you fill me in on what you think I don't know?" Curt Flanagan laughed.

David smiled. "So, you know what I'm going to say. I should have realized you have eyes, and you are around this community. So, what's your advice?"

"Let's not assume I know your feelings. I am aware that you and Rylee have become close friends and your children enjoy each other's company. I also know you lost your wife a few years ago and that you've been grieving. You've lived in our community for almost a year and seem to enjoy the church. Am I right, so far?"

"Yes, right on target. It was hard for me to move, but I had this job offer, and I couldn't turn it down. My family needed a smaller town, and my children needed me to be available when they needed me. Moving would allow that to happen. Then I met Rylee when I took Marcie to school that first day. I walked into her office and thought, what a lovely young lady. Her brown hair with the gold and blonde highlights and her big brown eyes just spoke to me. Such a sweet and innocent face."

"No one's perfect nor innocent, David. Now Rylee comes close, but not quite there. What else did you see?"

"Hurt, compassion, youth. I thought Rylee was about nineteen but knew she had to be older since she was the school nurse. Then later that day, I found her sitting with my youngest and a little boy and discovered she was a mom taking care of a young boy who had befriended my Susie. I was hooked."

"Have you given this relationship over to God?"

"Yes, sir."

"Then I'm not sure why you're here unless it's to get my permission or blessing. You and God will work this out. Talk to Rylee and tell her the same thing you told me."

"Some of it, but we just began to talk about what brought us to this part of our lives. We will have more discussions, I'm sure." David felt reassured now that he had spoken to the preacher.

Standing, the preacher put one hand on David's shoulder and asked God to bless him and to keep watch over David and Rylee as this friendship grew.

Walking out of the office, David felt a million bricks had lifted off his back.

A few days had passed since the picnic, and Rylee was still floating in the clouds. She liked David, really liked David. Rylee wanted him to feel the same way, but she needed to meet with the pastor. She needed his take and understanding of where she was and if this was the right thing to pursue.

Curt Flanagan looked at his appointments for the day and saw Rylee's name, and chuckled. It looked like they were both going at this the right way. He'd be happy to see her and listen to her thoughts.

Rylee walked into the pastor's office with confidence that he would be able to help her make a few decisions in this relationship.

She had prayed to God for His plan, but she didn't feel like her prayer was being answered. Sitting down, Pastor Flanagan shut the door and began.

"It's good to see you, Rylee. What can I do for you today? Are you here to volunteer as the Vacation Bible School coordinator?"

"That sounds wonderful, but I don't think so, Bro. Curt. I thought we already had a coordinator. Was I wrong?"

"No, it was my attempt at a joke!" he said, laughing with Rylee. "I thought that might put you at ease. Let's pray before we begin."

Rylee bowed her head as the preacher opened with prayer.

Then she began. "Oh, well, I wanted to talk about a relationship I want to build with David Hunt. We've known each other since September. You know he lost his wife over two years ago. I like him, I love his girls, and I want to make sure this is God's planning." Rylee kept on talking. "He is just about everything I could ask for in a man. My background isn't too good as far as men are concerned. I don't want to mess up this time. We've talked and shared, but we haven't made a commitment, and I don't know what we need to do next, but I know we need to talk to the kids. What do you think?"

The pastor laughed again, "Straight to the point! I like you, Rylee Abrams. You know who controls your life."

"God does, sir."

"Yes, and you are willing to let Him, so that's a good trait to have. Talk to each other. Tell him how you feel. Ask how he feels about making a commitment before God and each other to see where this relationship is going. Then . . . let God handle it. You'll be surprised what you learn."

"Thank you, Bro. Curt." Rylee rose to leave. "This wasn't as hard as I thought."

"See you in church Sunday." Pastor Flanagan said. "Maybe you can update me at that time."

"I will." Rylee felt good. Rylee felt as if a weight had been lifted after talking with the pastor. She couldn't wait to speak to David. Calling him, she asked him to come over for dinner that night and to bring the girls.

∞∞∞

That night after everyone had finished dinner, Marcie, Susie, and Tyler cleaned the table and put dishes in the dishwasher while Rylee and David took a walk.

David began, "I went to see the pastor this week."

"I did too. Why did you go to see him?"

"You tell me why you went." David didn't want to start. Rylee just looked at him. "All right. I wanted reassurance that if I pursue our relationship that what I was praying for was the right thing."

Rylee began laughing. "That's why I went to talk to him. Great minds think alike! I think it's important for us to sit the kids down and ask them if they have any problems with our dating, so to speak."

David began to feel a little uncomfortable. He wanted to see where the relationship would go, but telling the kids? "Do we need the kids involved? Isn't this adult stuff?"

"Yes, it is adult stuff. But they have been through a lot of trauma. If we date for a year and it goes nowhere, then they have to grieve again. Don't you think we should let them tell us if they want that or not?"

Stopping on the sidewalk, David turned her towards him. Looking into those brown eyes, he melted. "If we break up, I will grieve. I need you in my life, Rylee."

"Then let's go talk to the children. If they give the okay, then we can date. Sounds reasonable to me."

David leaned over and gave her a very light kiss. Rylee smiled.

Sitting the kids on the couch, seeing their confused faces like they were in trouble, Rylee assured them it was nothing terrible. David began, "I've had so much fun this school year getting to know Tyler and Rylee. How have you all felt?"

Marcie chimed in, "Me too. I feel like I now have a little brother and a good mommy role model in Rylee."

Susie yelled, "Me too! I have a mommy-person!"

Rylee picked up, "What about you, Tyler?"

"I think Susie and Marcie are my sisters. I can tell them anything, and they love me."

All three spoke at the same time, "Are you two getting married?"

David and Rylee looked shocked, "No, kids. We want to know if you have any problems with us dating for a while?"

"I don't care." Marcie piped up quickly.

"I don't either." Tyler and Susie were together on this.

"All right — let's have dessert!"

Rylee and David watched the three run into the kitchen and get ice cream. Looking at each other, David gently pushed her hair back and cupped his hand at the back of her neck. Pulling her closer, he gently lowered his lips to hers and sealed the deal. What or where would this relationship take them? They didn't know, but they would trust God's plan for their lives.

Epilogue

Love blossomed, trust grew, and a marriage happened in the summer one year later. Pastor Park married the two families uniting them into one. The wedding was held out by the pond where so many picnics and outings had helped this family to blossom and to grow close.

Clint had visited Tyler as much as possible, but he too had found happiness in another city, in another state and wasn't around much. He still called Tyler, but not as often.

Rylee and David had left Marcie, who would be in high school, to babysit Tyler and Susie while they took a short ride out to the pond.

"I brought some sandwiches and a blanket and some cold water," Rylee said to David. "I wasn't sure if we would stay very long, but I wanted a place for us to sit and food, if we got hungry."

"Good job, Mrs. Hunt!" David was still overjoyed at how Jesus had entered their lives and allowed them to find each other. They were deeply in love, and Rylee was all he could have asked for from God.

Sitting down on the blanket Rylee laid her head in David's lap. "You know I've been meaning to remind you today how very much I love you . . . I have a surprise. I hope it will help you understand my deep love for you."

David smiled and asked, "Lay it on me, sweetheart."

Rylee smiled and sat up. Sitting in his lap and putting her arms around him she whispered in his ear.

"What!?" David was overcome with pure excitement. "Does anyone else know?" Standing and pulling her up with him.

"Of course not silly. I only told you because you're the daddy!"

"When?"

"How does September sound?" Kissing they once again shared what God had started.

Books by Susan Bateman

To Capture a Heart
Apple Blossom Orchard

Books by S.B.Roth

It Happened One Christmas

Irish Legacy Series

Molly's Faith
Lily's Hope
Micah's Love

Waterstown Romance Series

An Unexpected Romance
A Chance Romance - Late 2021

The following titles may change
A Georgia Romance - Late 2021
It's Never Too Late - 2022
Love in a Small Town-2022

If you have read any of these books and enjoyed
please leave a review on Amazon.com